FUDGE-A-MANIA

Judy Blume

YEARLING BOOKS/YOUNG YEARLINGS/YEARLING CLASSICS are designed especially to entertain and enlighten young people. Patricia Reilly Giff, consultant to this series, received her bachelor's degree from Marymount College and a master's degree in history from St. John's University. She holds a Professional Diploma in Reading and a Doctorate of Humane Letters from Hofstra University. She was a teacher and reading consultant for many years, and is the author of numerous books for young readers.

For a complete listing of all Yearling titles, write to
Dell Readers Service
P.O. Box 1045
South Holland, IL 60473.

FUDGE-A-MANIA

Judy Blume

A Little Yearling Book

Published by
Dell Publishing
a division of
Bantam Doubleday Dell Publishing Group, Inc.
666 Fifth Avenue
New York, New York 10103

The author and publisher gratefully acknowledge permission to reprint the quoted passages on:

 page 42, from "Heigh-ho, Heigh-ho" from Walt Disney's *Snow White*. © Copyright 1938 by Bourne Co. (Renewed). Used by Permission of the Copyright Owner.

 pages 48, 77, 78, 138, and 144, from "Some Enchanted Evening" by Richard Rodgers and Oscar Hammerstein II. Copyright © 1949 by Richard Rodgers and Oscar Hammerstein II, copyright renewed. Williamson Music Co., owner of publication and allied rights. Used by permission. All rights reserved.

The trademark Yearling® is registered in the U.S. Patent and Trademark Office.

The trademark Dell® is registered in the U.S. Patent and Trademark Office.

ISBN: 0-440-70695-5

Reprinted by arrangement with Judy Blume, Inc.

Printed in the United States of America

September 1991

10 9 8 7 6 5 4 3 2 1

To George—who took me to Maine,
and was there to encourage me every day
and
to Larry—the original Fudge,
currently a member of the I.S.A.F. Club

Contents

Who's the Lucky Bride?

"Guess what, Pete?" my brother, Fudge, said. "I'm getting married tomorrow."

I looked up from my baseball cards. "Isn't this kind of sudden?" I asked, since Fudge is only five.

"No," he said.

"Well . . . who's the lucky bride?"

"Sheila Tubman," Fudge said.

I hit the floor, pretending to have fainted dead away. I did a good job of it because Fudge started shaking me and shouting, "Get up, Pete!"

What's with this Pete *business?* I thought. *Ever since he could talk, he's called me* Pee-tah.

Then Tootsie, my sister, who's just a year and a half, danced around me singing, "Up, Pee . . . up."

Next, Mom was beside me saying, "Peter . . . what happened? Are you all right?"

"I told him I was getting married," Fudge said. "And he just fell over."

"I fell over when you told me *who* you were marrying," I said.

"Who are you marrying, Fudge?" Mom asked, as if we were seriously discussing his wedding.

"Sheila Tubman," Fudge said.

"Don't say that name around me," I told him, "or I'll faint again."

"Speaking of Sheila Tubman . . ." Mom began.

But I didn't wait for her to finish. "You're making me feel very sick . . ." I warned.

"Really, Peter . . ." Mom said. "Aren't you overdoing it?"

I clutched my stomach and moaned but Mom went right on talking. "Buzz Tubman is the one who told us about the house in Maine."

"*M-a-i-n-e* spells *Maine,*" Fudge sang.

Mom looked at him but didn't even pause. "And this house is right next to the place they've rented for their vacation," she told me.

"I'm missing something here," I said. "What house? What vacation?"

"Remember we decided to go away for a few weeks in August?"

"Yeah . . . so?"

"So we got a great deal on a house in Maine."

"And the Tubmans are going to be next door?" I couldn't believe this. "Sheila Tubman . . . next door . . . for two whole weeks?"

"Three," Mom said.

I fell back flat on the floor.

"He did it again, Mom!" Fudge said.

"He's just pretending," Mom told Fudge. "He's just being very silly."

"So I don't have to marry Sheila tomorrow," Fudge said. "I'll marry her in Maine."

"That makes more sense," Mom said. "In Maine you can have a nice wedding under the trees."

"Under the trees," Fudge said.

"Tees . . ." Tootsie said, throwing a handful of Gummi Bears in my face.

And that's how it all began.

Pete and Farley

That night we went to Tico-Taco for supper. I wasn't very hungry. The idea of spending three weeks next door to Sheila Tubman was enough to take away my appetite. I wish the Tubmans would move to another planet! But until that happens there's no way to avoid Sheila. She lives in our apartment building. We go to the same school.

I kind of groaned and Dad looked at me. "What is it, Peter?"

"Sheila Tubman," I said.

"What about her?" Dad asked.

"We're getting married," Fudge said, his mouth full of chicken and taco shell.

"I'm not talking about your wedding," I said. "I'm talking about spending three weeks in Maine next door to the Tubmans."

"It won't be as bad as you think," Mom said.

"You don't know how bad I *think* it will be!"

"Sheila's older now. She's finished sixth grade, same as you."

"What's age got to do with it?" I said. "She'll still be the Queen of Cooties."

"What's *cooties?*" Fudge asked.

When I didn't answer he tugged on my sleeve. "What's *cooties*, Pete?"

"Since when am I *Pete?*" I asked, shaking him off.

"Since today," he said.

"Well, I prefer Peter, if you don't mind."

"Pete is a better name for a big brother."

"And Farley is a better name for a little brother!" I figured that would shut him up since his real name is Farley Drexel Hatcher and he's ready to kill anybody who calls him that.

"Don't call me Farley!" he said. Then he really let go and yelled, "I'm *Fudge!*"

The waiter, who heard him from across the room, came over to our table and said, "Sorry . . . we don't have any tonight. But we do have mud pie, which is almost the same thing."

7

Dad had to explain that we weren't talking about dessert. And Mom added, "We never eat dessert until we've finished our main course."

"Oh," the waiter said.

But before he had a chance to get away, Fudge looked up at him and said, "Do you have cooties?"

"Cooties?" the waiter asked. "For dessert?" He looked confused. Especially when Tootsie banged her spoon against the tray of her baby seat and sang, "Coo-tee . . . coo-tee . . ."

I could tell Fudge was about to ask the same question *again*, but before he had the chance I clamped my hand over his mouth. Then Dad told the waiter we didn't need anything else right now.

The waiter walked away shaking his head and I took my hand away from Fudge's mouth. As soon as I did, he was back in business. "What's *cooties?*" This time the people at the next table looked over at us.

"They're like nits," Mom told him, quietly.

"What's *nits?*" Fudge asked.

"Head lice," Dad said, almost in a whisper.

"Head mice?" Fudge asked.

"Not mice, Turkey Brain," I told him. "*Lice.* Little creepy, crawly bugs that live in hair." I snapped my fingernails at his head the way Sheila Tubman used to do to me.

Fudge yelled, "I don't want creepy, crawly bugs in my hair!"

Now everyone in the restaurant looked over at us.

"That's enough, Peter," Dad said.

"Well, he's the one who wanted to know."

"That's *enough*," Mom said. It came out sounding like *eee-nuff*, which got Tootsie going.

"Eee-eee-eee-eee . . ." Tootsie shrieked, banging her spoon.

This is the way it's going to be all summer, I thought, *only worse*. So I put down my taco and said, "Maybe I should go to camp in August."

Dad got this really serious look on his face. "We don't have the money this year, Peter. We wouldn't be going away at all if it weren't for Grandma, who's paying more than her share."

"But if you want, you can bring a friend," Mom said.

"A friend?" I asked. "You mean like Jimmy Fargo?" They both nodded.

Jimmy is my best friend in New York. We've always wanted to spend the summer together.

"What about me?" Fudge asked. "Can I bring a friend, too?"

I held my breath.

"You'll find a friend in Maine," Mom told him.

"Suppose I don't?" Fudge asked.

"You're getting married," I reminded him.

"Does that mean I don't get a friend?" Fudge asked.

"Of course not," Mom told him. "I'm married and I have friends. Daddy's married and he has friends."

"What about Uncle Feather?" I said. Uncle Feather is Fudge's myna bird. "He's your friend, isn't he?"

"I can't play with Uncle Feather," Fudge said. "He's not that kind of friend. And I can't marry him either. If he was a girl bird it would be different."

"People don't marry birds," I told him.

"Some people do."

"Name one," I said.

"The guy who's married to Big Bird on *Sesame Street.*"

"Big Bird's not married," I said.

"That's how much you know!" Fudge shouted. He's learned to say that every time someone disagrees with him. It's a real conversation stopper. "I give up!" I said, going back to my taco, which was getting soggy.

"Up," Tootsie repeated, holding out her arms. "Up . . . up . . . up."

Dad lifted her out of the baby seat and she squirmed until he put her down. Then she took off, toddling through the restaurant, stopping at every table. Fudge scrambled off his chair and ran after her. Eating out with my family is not exactly relaxing.

"Here, girl . . ." Fudge said, as if he were calling a dog. "Here's something just for you." He lured her back to our table and dropped some of his taco on her tray. "Yum . . ." he said to her. "Yum . . . yum . . . yum . . ."

Dad put Tootsie back into her seat. She stuffed the chicken pieces into her mouth.

"I always know what Tootsie wants," Fudge said. "That's why I'm her favorite brother."

"Tootsie doesn't have favorites," Mom told him. "She loves both her brothers."

"But she loves me best!" Fudge said. Then he looked at me and laughed. When he did, half the food in his mouth wound up on my shirt.

I called Jimmy Fargo as soon as we got home. I asked him to come to Maine with us.

"Three weeks next door to Sheila Tubman?"

"The houses are really far apart," I said. Nobody told me this but I was hoping it was true. "You won't even be able to see her house. There'll probably be a forest separating us."

When he didn't say anything I added, "And don't forget . . . Sheila's scared of dogs so we can get Turtle after her anytime she tries to give us trouble." Turtle is my dog. He's big enough to look scary but he'd never hurt anybody. Lucky for us, Sheila doesn't know that.

Jimmy laughed. "Maybe I can come for a week."

"A week isn't long enough!"

"Hey, Peter . . . no offense . . . but a week with your family can feel like a long time."

That's because Jimmy's the only kid in his family. His parents are divorced. He lives with his father, Frank Fargo, who's a painter.

"How about two weeks?" I said.

"Is your brother bringing his bird?"

"Yeah . . . Uncle Feather's part of the family," I told him. "Same as Turtle."

"So it will be your mother, your father, Fudge, Tootsie, Turtle, Uncle Feather and you?"

"Right," I said. "And my grandmother's coming too."

"The one who taught you to stand on your head?"

"Yeah." Grandma Muriel is Mom's mother. She ran a gymnastics camp before she retired.

"You think she could teach me?" Jimmy asked.

"Maybe," I said.

"I'll talk to my father," Jimmy said. "I'll let you know tomorrow."

He called back the next morning. Mr. Fargo liked the idea of Maine. He liked it so much he said he'd drive Jimmy up and camp out in the area himself.

"That's great!" I said. Maybe three weeks in Maine wouldn't be as bad as I'd thought.

3

The Most Disgusting of Them All

It took ten hours to drive to Southwest Harbor, Maine. Ten hours in the backseat of an old Blazer with Fudge, Tootsie, Turtle and Uncle Feather, who wouldn't shut up. Some myna birds don't talk at all but Uncle Feather's not one of them. He'll repeat anything you say. Finally, I dropped the cover over his cage, hoping he'd think it was nighttime. "Go to sleep, stupid!" I told him. *Stupid* is one of his favorite words.

But that didn't work either. "Go to sleep, stupid . . ." he chanted, until even Turtle lost patience and started barking. *Grandma is really smart,* I thought. *She's flying up to Maine.*

As we got closer to our destination, Mom started reading to us from a guidebook. "Southwest Harbor is on an island called Mount Desert." She pronounced it de-*sert.*

"Ice cream, cookies, brownies, pudding . . ." Fudge sang.

Mom kept right on reading. I don't know why she thinks Fudge pays any attention to her lectures on history. He hears only what he wants to hear. Everything else goes right by him.

"Founded in 1905, the town of Southwest Harbor . . ." *You call this a town?* I thought, as we drove through it. There was one street with a couple of shops. And that was about it. But I could tell Mom was really excited. She put down her guidebook and smiled at my father. "Oh, it's so quaint," she said. "Isn't it quaint, Warren?"

And my father smiled back and said, "It's perfect, honey."

Fudge chucked Tootsie under her chin. "It's perfect, honey," he said, imitating my father.

Then Uncle Feather started. *"Honey . . . honey . . . honey."* For some reason Tootsie thought that was wildly funny, and she laughed until she got the hiccups. Mom passed a bottle of water to the backseat and I stuck it in Tootsie's mouth.

"Take a left here, Warren," Mom said to Dad. We turned onto a dirt road, then pulled into a gravel driveway and parked in front of an old, weathered wood house. The first person I saw was the Queen of Cooties herself. She was standing on the seat of a rope swing. It hung from the branch of a big tree in the front yard.

She was swinging pretty high when I opened the back door of the Blazer and Turtle jumped out. It had been almost four hours since I'd walked him and he really had to go. He raced for the woods behind the house but Sheila thought he was heading straight for her.

"Help!" she screamed, wobbling on the swing. "Somebody please heeelp!" She lost her balance and fell to the ground. *What a dork!*

Mom jumped out of the car and ran to her rescue. "It's all right," she said, helping Sheila to her feet. "Turtle just had to wee-wee." How could Mom have used such an embarrassing expression?

By then Mr. and Mrs. Tubman, who had also heard Sheila's screams, came running out of the house. "Are you okay?" Mrs. Tubman asked Sheila.

"I'm fine," Sheila said, brushing herself off. "It was just that *disgusting* dog!"

Before I had the chance to tell her who was *really* disgusting, a man with white hair called,

"Lemonade . . ." We all headed for the house and gathered around the table on the porch. "I'm Buzz Tubman's father," the white-haired man said. He poured each of us a glass of lemonade. "Call me Buzzy Senior."

I polished off my drink really fast. Buzzy Senior poured me another. I gulped it down. "Long trip up here, isn't it?" he asked.

"Ten hours," I said, wiping my mouth with the back of my hand. He filled my glass again.

I didn't even notice Fudge watching until then. "You must be really thirsty, Pete."

"Yeah," I said.

"Remember that time you drank too much Island Punch and you . . ."

I clamped my hand over his mouth. He still doesn't get the difference between stories you tell to strangers and stories you keep to yourself. I looked at Buzzy Senior. "Fudge knows a lot about dinosaurs," I said, hoping to change the subject.

But as soon as I took my hand away from his mouth Fudge laughed. "And Pete knows all about cooties."

"Well, you can't know too much about cooties, can you, Pete?" Buzzy Senior said, smiling at me.

"And guess what else?" Fudge said. "I'm getting married under the trees."

"Do I know the bride?" Buzzy Senior asked.

"It's Sheila Tubman!" Fudge said.

"Oh, my granddaughter," Buzzy Senior said.

"Sheila's your granddaughter?" Fudge asked.

Buzzy Senior nodded. "Have you popped the question yet?"

"How do you *pop* a question?" Fudge said.

"You have to ask if she *wants* to marry you," Buzzy Senior explained.

"Why wouldn't she want to marry me?"

"It's something you have to decide together," Buzzy Senior said.

"Okay . . ." Fudge said. He turned toward Sheila, who was sitting in a rocking chair. "Hey, Sheila . . . you want to marry me . . . right?"

Sheila laughed so hard she nearly fell off the chair.

"See . . ." Fudge said. "I popped the question and she wants to marry me."

"Congratulations," Buzzy Senior said. "You're a lucky man."

Lucky? I thought. That's not what I'd call it.

The screen door opened and Libby stepped out onto the porch. Libby is Sheila's older sister. She's almost sixteen but no one would make the mistake of calling her *sweet*. She was carrying a small white-and-brown puppy.

Sheila jumped. I expected her to run for her life. Instead, she cooed, "Oooh . . . my baby . . .

my precious furry baby . . ." She kissed the puppy about twenty times.

"You have a dog?" I asked.

"Yes," Sheila said proudly. "Her name is Jake and we just got her. Isn't she adorable?"

"I thought you're afraid of dogs."

"She is," Libby said.

"I'm *not* afraid of Jake!"

"She's afraid of dogs, in general," Libby told me.

"That is sooo unfair!" Sheila said.

"But it's true, isn't it?" Libby asked in her most obnoxious voice.

"I just don't like big, smelly, *disgusting* dogs," Sheila said, looking directly at me.

"Are you calling *my* dog smelly and disgusting?" I asked.

Sheila folded her arms and smiled. "Turtle is the *most* disgusting dog ever born!"

"You want to see disgusting . . . look in the mirror," I told her. "You want to smell disgusting . . . smell yourself!"

"Are you two going to argue for three weeks?" Libby asked. "Because that could get to be a real bore."

"You're right," I said. "So why don't you just tell me where *our* house is and that'll be the end of it."

"This *is* your house," Sheila said.

"I thought this was *your* house."

"It's *two* houses, but they're connected."

"What do you mean *connected?*" I asked.

"Didn't you learn anything in sixth grade, Peter? *Connected* means attached . . . joined together . . ."

"I *know* what the word means," I told her.

"Don't worry," Sheila said, "there's an inside door that separates your house from ours."

An inside door? I thought. *How am I going to explain this to Jimmy Fargo? I promised him a forest between our houses . . . not an inside door!*

Suddenly we heard a rustling sound and a minute later Turtle came tearing out of the woods. A terrible smell followed him. I mean *really* bad.

"Eeeuuuw . . ." Sheila cried, holding her nose. "Whath that thmell?"

"Ith thkunk!" Dad said, holding his. "Turtle'th been thprayed by a thkunk."

"Oh no!" Mom said. She held her nose, too. "Not thkunk!"

They all sounded as if they had the worst colds. I would have laughed, except for the smell. It was so strong I had to hold my nose, just like the rest of them.

"Thith ith too nautheating for wordth!" Libby said, grabbing Jake and running back into the house.

"Do thomething, Peter!" Sheila yelled.

"What am I thuppoth to do?"

"He'th *your* dog, ithn't he?"

"Leth not panic," Mr. Tubman said. "Leth think thith through in a logical way."

"Thith ithn't the time for logic!" Mrs. Tubman said. "Thith ith the time for action!"

"Tomato juith!" Buzzy Senior said. "Put him in a tub of tomato juith."

"Where am I thuppoth to get enough tomato juith to cover him?" Mrs. Tubman asked.

"I'll take care of it, Jean!" Dad said. "Don't worry." He headed for the Blazer.

Fudge chased Dad. "Wait for me!"

"Where are you going, Warren?" Mom called.

"For tomato juith!" Dad called back.

All this time Turtle was rolling over and over in the grass, trying to get rid of the awful smell. He knew he was in big trouble.

"I alwayth knew your dog wath the thmellieth dog in the entire world," Sheila said. "And thith provth it!"

For once I had to agree.

The Worst News of the Century

I wasn't surprised that our first hour in Maine was a disaster. I knew if Sheila Tubman was involved it would be. I begged Mom and Dad to leave right after Dad scrubbed Turtle with this special shampoo called Skunked. But by then, hamburgers were cooking on the grill. So I begged them to leave right after supper. But they wouldn't listen.

"Don't say I didn't warn you!" I told them.

"I guess we're willing to take our chances," Dad said. "Now let's get some sleep. It's been a long day."

We carried our bags through the inside door separating our house from Sheila's. But on the other side there was just a staircase leading to three bedrooms and one bathroom.

"This is it?" I said. "This is our *house?*"

"Yes," Mom said. "Isn't it nice?"

"Where's the living room?" I asked. "Where's the kitchen?"

"We're sharing the living room and kitchen with the Tubmans," Dad said.

"Sharing!" I could hardly get the word out. "We're *sharing* with the Tubmans?"

"Learn to share," Fudge said, "and you'll be a very happy person."

"Don't give me any of your kindergarten philosophy," I told him. "This is serious!"

Upstairs, Mom and Dad looked over the three bedrooms. They chose the one with the double bed for themselves. The second bedroom had a single bed plus a crib. Grandma would share that with Tootsie. Which left the smallest bedroom for Fudge and me. "You two should be comfortable in here," Dad said.

I looked around. There were two camp beds so close together you could kick the person in the other bed. *That should be useful if Fudge talks in his sleep,* I thought. There was also a lamp and a low chest with two drawers. And the ceiling sloped on one side of the room so when I stood up straight I banged my head on it.

"What about when Jimmy comes?" I asked Mom.

"We'll work it out," she said. "Don't worry."

But how could I *not* worry?

At least Mom was able to convince Fudge that Uncle Feather would be happier downstairs. "We'll put his cage in front of the picture window in the living room so he can watch what's happening," she said.

"Suppose he has a bad dream?" Fudge said.

"Does he usually have dreams?" Mom asked, as if Fudge were an expert.

"Sometimes he dreams of scary monsters," Fudge said, "especially if he has to sleep all alone in a strange place."

"When you cover his cage he won't know he's in a strange place," I said.

"He'll know," Fudge said.

"He's a very well-adjusted bird," I argued. "He'll be fine." I wasn't about to share a room with Fudge *and* Uncle Feather.

Even Fudge was too tired to argue. "Okay," he said, yawning. Then he flopped on his bed and was out cold before I turned off the light.

We went to town the next afternoon. The gears on Dad's bike were stuck so he dropped it off at Bicycle Bob's shop for repairs. Bicycle

Bob is a big, friendly guy who wears a T-shirt that says *I'd Rather Be Biking*. Then we went to Sawyer's Market for groceries and to the library to get our cards and to Oz Books, where Fudge and I each got two paperbacks. After that we headed for the airport.

Grandma's plane was right on time. As soon as we got home she shook hands with each of the Tubmans and said, "Call me Muriel." Then she turned four cartwheels on the front lawn. I could tell the Tubmans were impressed.

"Muriel . . ." Sheila called, chasing Grandma. "Could you teach me to turn cartwheels?"

"I don't see why not," Grandma said, breathing hard. "I ran a gymnastics camp for years."

"Oh, I'd just love to turn cartwheels," Sheila gushed. "My friend Mouse Ellis can turn cartwheels."

"You have a friend named *Mouse?*" I asked.

"Mouse . . . mice . . . creepy, crawly lice," Fudge sang, pleased with his rhyme.

"Fudgie!" Sheila scolded. "That's not exactly nice!" Then she turned back to me with her hands on her hips. "My friend Mouse is coming here in ten days."

"But that's when Jimmy Fargo's coming!" I heard my voice crack but I didn't care.

"Jimmy Fargo's coming here?" Sheila's voice sounded funny, too.

"Yeah . . . for a week . . . at least."

"That's the worst news of the century!" Sheila cried.

"The worst news of the century," Fudge said, doing a perfect imitation of Sheila. "The worst news of the century . . ."

"Stop that, Fudgie!" Sheila picked him up and shook him.

"Is that any way to treat your future husband?" I asked.

"Yeah . . ." Fudge said. "Mommy never shakes Dad."

"We're never getting married if you act that way!" Sheila told him. "Say you're sorry or the wedding's off."

"Are you going to let her boss you around like that?" I asked Fudge.

"Just stay out of this, Peter!" Sheila said.

"Yeah, Pete," Fudge said.

"Fine," I told him. "You want to cook your own goose . . . go ahead."

Fudge started laughing. "I don't have a goose, Pete."

Uncle Feather's Adventure

The next day, when I got up, Fudge's bed was empty. He doesn't know you're supposed to sleep late when you're on vacation. I pulled on my jeans, which I'd left on the floor. They felt cold and damp. I forgot about the sloped ceiling until I stood up and whacked my head. That made me so mad I kicked the wall. So before the day even started, I had a bump on my head and a pain in my foot. As I pulled on my sweatshirt, I heard foghorns in the distance. I took a look out the window. Nothing but white. We were completely fogged in.

I hope Grandma's making cocoa, I thought, on my way downstairs. She likes to get up early. She says at her age you really appreciate morning and there's no point in wasting it. So I wasn't surprised to hear her laughing as I came through the inside door.

The kitchen and the living room are really one big room, with a stone fireplace in the center. Buzzy Senior was having breakfast with Grandma. They'd really hit it off last night. At supper they'd laughed so hard you'd have thought they were old friends.

At the same time, Grandma was trying to feed Tootsie oatmeal. But Tootsie likes to feed herself so she grabbed the spoon out of Grandma's hand and wound up with a blob of oatmeal in her hair.

"Pee," Tootsie said, when she spotted me.

"You have to go potty?" Grandma asked, as if Tootsie is toilet trained, which she definitely is not.

"She's trying to say *Pete*," Fudge explained. He was at the table counting Cheerios. He counts out exactly two hundred before he starts to eat. It takes forever because half the time he gets his numbers mixed up. Mom says it's just another phase and he'll get over it. He better or he'll never make it to school on time.

Then Sheila waltzed in wearing a fuzzy pink robe and bunny slippers. You'd think she'd be embarrassed to be seen that way but I guess nothing embarrasses the Cootie Queen. When Jimmy finds out he has to see *her* first thing in the morning he'll be on the next plane back to New York.

Sheila opened all the windows in the living room on her way to the table.

"What are you doing, Sheila?" Grandma said. "You're freezing us out."

"I can't *stand* the smell," Sheila said.

"It's a Maine smell," Buzzy Senior said. "It's the dampness and the mildew."

"Doggie-do is more like it!" Sheila said.

"Maybe *your* dog goes inside but my dog doesn't!" I told her.

"Close the windows, Sheila, please . . ." Grandma said. "The baby could catch a chill."

Sheila muttered to herself but she closed the windows. When she got to the one in front of Uncle Feather's cage she peered inside and said, "Where's your bird, Fudge?"

"What do you mean?" I asked.

"I mean . . . Uncle Feather's not in his cage," Sheila said.

I looked over at Fudge but he kept counting his Cheerios. "Eighty-two . . . eighty-three . . ."

"His bird is gone?" I asked.

"Yes," Sheila said. "Gone . . . as in *not present* . . . as in *disappeared from view* . . ."

I jumped up from the table and ran over to Uncle Feather's cage. Sheila was right. Uncle Feather was definitely *not present*.

I looked back at Fudge, who kept counting his Cheerios. "Eighty-four, eighty-five . . ."

"Where's Uncle Feather?" I asked him.

"Someplace nice," he said. "Eighty-six . . ."

"What does that mean?" I said.

"I'm trying to count!"

"I'm waiting for an answer," I told him. So was everyone else.

Finally Fudge looked up from his Cheerios. "He was bored. He wanted to come out of his cage."

"You let him out of his cage?" I couldn't believe this.

"Just for a little while." He started counting again. "Fifty-two, fifty-three . . ."

"Go get him!" I said.

"First I'll have my cereal."

"Oh no you won't," I told him. "First you'll get your bird."

"Grandma . . ." Fudge said in his best little-boy voice.

But Grandma didn't fall for it. "Go and get your bird, Fudge. Your cereal will wait."

Buzzy Senior and Grandma exchanged a long look as Fudge ran out of the room and headed up the stairs on the Tubmans' side of the house. Then they laughed. But I didn't see anything funny. I sat down and buttered a piece of toast.

In a couple of minutes Fudge was back. "He's not there."

"Not where?" I asked.

"Not where I left him."

"Where did you leave him?"

"I can't tell . . . but he's not there anymore. And the window's open."

I looked over at Sheila.

"Well, how was I supposed to know his bird wasn't in its cage?" she said.

"You opened the windows everywhere?" I asked.

"Well, yes . . . because of the smell."

I shoved my chair back from the table.

"Let's not panic," Sheila said, sounding exactly like her father. "Let's think this through in a logical way."

"I've thought it through," I told her. I grabbed my rain jacket from the hook near the front door. "Come on," I called to Fudge.

"Search and Rescue," Buzzy Senior said. "That's the spirit." He raised his coffee cup to toast us.

I helped Fudge into his new yellow slicker.

It's so long it hangs down to the ground, making him look like a little old man with no feet. I stuck the matching hat on his head.

"Be careful boys," Grandma called. "It's very foggy out there."

"Wait!" Sheila said. "I'll get dressed and come with you."

"Forget it," I told her.

"You're making a big mistake," she said. "Because *I'm* the one who noticed the empty cage."

"Yeah . . . and *you're* the one who opened all the windows!" I pushed Fudge out the door and let it slam behind me.

Outside the fog was so thick you couldn't even see the cars parked in our driveway. It was like standing inside a big white cloud.

"Where do birds go when it's foggy?" Fudge asked.

"If they're smart they stay home!"

We walked along a path through the woods, calling to Uncle Feather. *"Where are you, stupid?"* We used all his favorite expressions but he didn't answer. There was no sound except for the foghorn in the distance.

"Uncle Feather's just playing a game . . . right?" Fudge asked.

"Let's hope."

The path led us down to the water. There were a couple of houses overlooking the harbor. But it was too foggy to see any of the boats.

"We'll start here," I told Fudge, stopping in front of an old white house with black shutters. We climbed the steps to the front porch.

"I'll talk," Fudge said. "He's my bird."

"Okay . . . but don't waste a lot of time." I rang the bell.

A woman about Grandma's age came to the door. "Have you seen Uncle Feather?" Fudge asked, getting right to the point.

"Uncle who?" she said.

"Uncle Feather," Fudge repeated.

"Why, no . . . at least I don't think so . . . but come in out of that fog and tell me all about him." We followed her to the kitchen. "You can call me Mrs. A," she told us. "My husband and I live here all year round. Where are you boys staying?"

"Through the woods," Fudge said. "We have a swing."

"Oh, yes . . . I've noticed a whole gang at that house."

"There's Mommy and Daddy and Tootsie and Grandma," Fudge said, ticking off names on his fingers. "And Buzzy Senior, Sheila, Libby, Mr. and Mrs. Tubman . . . and Turtle, Jake,

Uncle Feather . . . and me and my brother, Pete. This is Pete," he said, pointing at me. "He's not supposed to talk."

Mrs. A looked at me. "That sore throat is going around," she said. "I had it myself last week. What you need is some hot tea with lemon and honey."

Before I had the chance to explain that my throat wasn't sore, Fudge made himself comfortable at the kitchen table. "Something smells good," he said.

Mrs. A set out a plate of cinnamon buns. "Fresh from the oven," she told him. "And I'll bet you could use a nice hot cup of cocoa, too."

"I could," Fudge said. "I didn't have any breakfast."

"Why, that's terrible," Mrs. A said. "On a morning like this you need a big, hot breakfast."

I tugged at the sleeve of Fudge's slicker, reminding him that we didn't have time to waste if we were going to find Uncle Feather. But he ignored me.

Mrs. A poured Fudge a cup of cocoa. Then she poured me a cup of tea. She stirred in a spoon of honey and squeezed in the juice from a lemon wedge. "That should fix your sore throat," she said. I didn't tell her that when I'm sick I like Mo's Herb Tea. Or that Fudge's cocoa smelled so good I could feel my mouth watering. There are times when it's better not to say anything.

Mrs. A joined us at the table. She helped herself to a cinnamon bun. "I can't resist them," she explained with a guilty look on her face.

"This is good cocoa," Fudge said, slurping it with a spoon.

"Thank you," Mrs. A said. "Mitzi says my cocoa's the best."

"Who's Mitzi?" Fudge asked.

"My granddaughter. She's five."

"I'm five, too," Fudge said.

"Well, you'll have to come by and meet her. She'll be here tomorrow."

"Okay," Fudge said. "I'm getting married soon but I can still have friends . . . right?"

"That's right," Mrs. A said. "Everybody needs friends." She didn't ask Fudge about getting married. Instead she watched, fascinated, as he unwound his cinnamon bun and picked out all the raisins. He piled them up in the corner of his plate.

Finally Mrs. A said, "I certainly hope your uncle's not out sailing in this weather."

"I hope not, too," Fudge said. "Because he doesn't know how to sail."

"Oh dear."

"He's not even supposed to go outside."

"This sounds serious," she said. "Have you called the police?"

"Not yet," Fudge said. "We called the Search and Rescue team."

"Are they coming soon?" she asked him.

"They're already here," he told her.

"That's a relief," she said. "What does your uncle look like . . . in case I see someone who fits his description?"

"He's mostly black with yellow feet and a yellow nose," Fudge said, stuffing the last of the cinnamon bun into his mouth.

Mrs. A seemed surprised by Fudge's description. I could tell she was thinking hard. Then her face lit up and she waved her hands around. "Oh . . . I get it. Your uncle's a scuba diver."

"Does Uncle Feather know how to dive?" Fudge asked me.

"I'm not sure," I said, getting up from the table, "but we've really got to go if we're going to find him."

When we got to the front door, Mrs. A took me aside and whispered, "Is your uncle all right . . . upstairs?" She tapped the side of her head in case I didn't get her point.

"Hard to say," I whispered back. Then I shoved Fudge out the front door. "Thanks for the snack."

"Come back tomorrow," Mrs. A called.

"Okay," Fudge said.

As soon as we were away from the house, I grabbed Fudge by the arm. "Why didn't you tell her Uncle Feather's a bird?"

"She knows that!" Fudge said.

"How does she know?"

"Everybody knows Uncle Feather's a bird."

"No . . . she thinks he's your *uncle.*"

"My *uncle,*" Fudge said, laughing. "That's really stupid!"

"Right. That's why you should have told her. She thinks there's this guy running around in a black wet suit with yellow flippers and a yellow face mask . . . this guy who's a little weird upstairs . . ." I tapped the side of my head the way Mrs. A had. "And that he's your uncle."

"Come on, Pete!"

"That's what she thinks. She doesn't know Uncle Feather's a myna bird because you didn't tell her. You have to give the facts. You have to say, *My myna bird is missing. He's mostly black with yellow feet and a yellow bill.* Not *nose,*" I told him. "People have noses. Birds have bills. Get it?"

"She made good cocoa."

"If you stop for cocoa at every house we're never going to find him."

"Never?"

"Never!"

Fudge started crying.

"That's not going to help." I dragged him along the rocky beach, hoping we'd hear Uncle Feather calling to us. But there was no sound except the waves breaking against the rocks.

We went to three more houses along the water and Fudge made it clear that his myna bird was missing. But no one had seen Uncle Feather, although they all promised to keep a lookout for him. So we trudged back to our house.

Sheila was watching for us at the living room window. She opened the door. "Did you find him?" she asked.

"No," I said.

Fudge sniffled. Then he covered his face with his hands and lay down on the floor, still wearing his yellow slicker and rain hat.

We were quiet for a while. I guess all three of us were thinking about Uncle Feather—alone, lost and frightened.

Suddenly, we heard a piercing scream. Fudge jumped up and grabbed Sheila. I dashed to the hall closet, looking for something to use as a weapon, just in case. But before I could even grab an umbrella we heard another scream. This time Sheila and Fudge crawled under the table. Then Libby tore through the house, yelling, "Heeelp . . . there's a bat after me!" She raced around the living room.

There was more noise and confusion as Libby bumped into furniture and knocked over a lamp. Not that she stopped for a minute! She kept screeching and running in circles. I heard the sound of flapping wings. When I looked up I saw something black flying after Libby. That's when I realized Libby wasn't the only one screeching. "Stop!" I shouted. But Libby didn't listen. "That's no bat," I yelled as I started running after her. "That's Uncle Feather!"

"My bird?" Fudge called, from under the table.

"Yes, Turkey Brain . . . your bird!"

Fudge and Sheila came out of hiding and joined the chase.

It didn't take long before everyone else in the house came to see what was happening.

Tootsie, who's a good screecher herself, joined right in. "Eeee . . . eeeee . . . eeeeeee!" She screeched as loud as she could, which got Uncle Feather going again.

"You four are going to have to play more quietly," Mrs. Tubman said.

"We're not playing!" Libby screamed.

"Eeee . . . eeeee . . . eeeeeee . . ." Tootsie kept it up.

"Everybody *freeze!*" Dad shouted. "Just freeze right where you are."

Libby froze. I crashed into her, Fudge crashed into me, Sheila crashed into Fudge.

Uncle Feather flew across the room. He perched on top of his cage and looked over at us. "Stupid . . . stupid . . . stupid . . ." he called. Then he hopped into his cage and Buzzy Senior closed the door.

We untangled ourselves. Sheila looked at me. "All's well that ends well . . . right, Peter?"

"Yeah, Pete . . ." Fudge said. "All's well that ends well." Then he turned two somersaults and landed in my lap.

The Perfect Baby-Sitter

The next morning, Sheila cornered my mother on the porch. She had the brilliant idea that she should baby-sit Fudge and that Mom should pay her.

"Look at it this way, Mrs. Hatcher," Sheila said, making her case. "You're always worrying about him, right? You never know what he might do. And this is supposed to be your vacation. Wouldn't it be nice if you could relax?"

"Remember the last time Sheila baby-sat Fudge?" I told Mom. "Remember how he lost his two front teeth trying to fly off the monkey bars?"

"That was years ago, Mrs. Hatcher," Sheila said. "Fudge wasn't even three. And I took a baby-sitting course this year. I guarantee satisfaction."

"No baby-sitting course could prepare you for Fudge!" I argued.

But Mom wasn't listening to me. She said, "I think you have a good point, Sheila. I *would* be more relaxed with someone looking after Fudge."

"Who ever heard of a wife baby-sitting her husband?" I asked.

"Everyone knows this marriage thing is a joke," Sheila said. "Everyone except you, Peter!"

"Yeah . . . what about the groom? He thinks it's for real."

"Seven dollars a day," Mom said to Sheila. "Two hours in the morning and four in the afternoon. If we need you after supper, we'll pay extra."

"It's a deal," Sheila said, shaking Mom's hand. Then she skipped off singing, "Heigh-ho, heigh-ho, it's off to work we go . . ."

"What about me?" I asked Mom. "What am I supposed to do while she's baby-sitting Fudge?"

"Why, Peter . . ." Mom said. "I thought you'd welcome the chance to have some time to yourself."

"Yeah . . . once Jimmy Fargo gets here."

"Well . . . maybe you and Sheila can watch Fudge together until Jimmy comes."

"Together?"

"Yes, together."

"And you'll pay me, too?"

"I'm paying seven dollars a day," Mom said. "I don't care how you split it."

But Sheila wasn't interested in sharing her salary with me. "It was *my* idea," she said. "Why should I give up half my money?"

"Because he's too much for one person to handle."

"I can handle anything, Peter. I'm a very responsible person." She turned away from me and called, "Fudgie . . . where are you?"

"Up here, honey . . ." Fudge called back, in his best husband voice. He was sitting on a branch in the swing tree.

"What are you doing up there?" Sheila asked, standing under him.

"Resting," Fudge said. "A bird always rests after breakfast."

"I've got news for you," I told him. "You're not a bird."

"I'm practicing for when I grow up," he said.

"You're not going to be a bird when you grow up," I reminded him.

"I *know* I'm not going to be a bird," he said,

swinging his feet. "I'm going to be a bird breather."

"What's a bird breather?" Sheila asked.

"Somebody who breathes for birds."

"I never heard of that," Sheila said. "People don't breathe for birds."

"That's how much you know!"

Sheila looked at me.

"He means a bird *breeder*," I said. *Without me around she'll never understand him.*

"Oh . . . a bird breeder," Sheila said. "That makes more sense."

"What makes more sense?" Fudge asked.

"Being a bird breeder," Sheila said.

"What's a *breeder?*" Fudge asked.

"Someone who breeds birds and animals," Sheila said.

"What's *breeds?*"

Sheila looked at me again.

"*You* wanted to be in charge," I said. "*You* answer his questions."

"It's someone who raises animals," Sheila explained. "Like a dog breeder raises dogs and a cat breeder raises cats and a bird breeder raises birds."

"And a baby breeder raises babies?" Fudge asked.

"Not exactly," Sheila told him. "Parents raise babies."

"How come baby breeders don't raise babies?"

"I don't know!" Sheila said. "It just doesn't work that way."

I started to laugh. *Just wait till she finds out how many questions he asks a day!*

"Now come down from that tree!" Sheila told Fudge.

"No!"

"Very well," she said, sounding exactly like our fifth-grade teacher. She marched off toward the garage and came back with a ten-foot ladder. Just as she got it to the tree, Fudge scrambled down, fast as a squirrel. "Ha ha . . ." he sang. "Fooled you, didn't I?"

Sheila put her hands on his shoulders and her face right up close to his. "Now listen to me, Fudge Hatcher . . . I made a deal with your mother. I'm going to be your baby-sitter and you're . . ."

He didn't wait for her to finish. "I thought you're going to be my wife."

"First I'm going to be your baby-sitter," she said. "And if that works out we'll talk about the wedding!"

After lunch everyone went off to their afternoon activities, just like at summer camp. Libby went to work at Ickle's Ice Cream Parlor. Grandma and Buzzy Senior went for a hike in Acadia National Park. Mom and Dad took Tootsie to the pond to see the ducks. The Tubmans went to visit friends. And Sheila took Fudge down to the beach.

So for once there was no one around to bother me . . . no one to ask stupid questions. *This is the life*, I thought, as I stretched out in the hammock in the backyard. *I can do anything I feel like doing now. I can finish my Gary Paulsen book . . . or ride my bicycle out to the lighthouse . . .*

I looked over at Turtle, who was sleeping in the sun. I could tell he was having a dream by the way his legs and tail twitched. I thought about taking him for a walk. He could use the exercise. Since we got here he's been sleeping a lot. A walk to the beach would do him good. I jumped up and called, "Come on, boy . . . let's go have some fun!"

Turtle opened his eyes and looked at me. He yawned. "Don't you want to go to the beach?" I asked, tugging at his collar. But he still wouldn't budge.

"Okay . . . fine," I told him. "Just sit there!"

I walked away, sure he would follow me. But when I turned back to check he was asleep again. *Who cares?* I thought. *I don't need him. I don't need anyone. I can have plenty of fun on my own.*

I walked through the woods to the beach.

Sheila and Fudge were out in front of Mrs. A's house, rock hunting. What a joke! The whole beach is made of pink rocks. When the tide is out you can walk on rocks for miles.

I headed in their direction. At first they didn't notice me. They were too busy choosing rocks to dump in their bucket. So I snuck up right behind Sheila and made a loud barking sound. *Rrruuufff!*

Sheila jumped about three feet. She was really mad when she saw it was me. "Who invited you?" she shouted.

"It's a public beach," I told her. "I don't need an invitation."

"I want you to know, Peter Hatcher, that even if you spend all day, every day with us, you're still not getting a penny of my baby-sitting money!"

"I don't want your money!"

"Then what are you doing here?" she asked.

"Anyone who feels like being here can be here," I told her.

"So how come you didn't feel like being here before? How come you suddenly feel like it now?"

I spread my arms wide and sang as loud as I could. *"Who can explain it, who can tell you why?"*

Fudge started laughing.

"Don't encourage him!" Sheila said.

I kept on singing. *"Fools give you reasons, wise men never trrrrrrryyyyyyy . . ."* I learned that song last night, from Buzzy Senior and Grandma. It's called "Some Enchanted Evening."

"This is too embarrassing for words!" Sheila said.

I would have kept on singing, but Mrs. A called from her porch. "Yoo hoo . . . yoo hoo, boys . . ." She waved to us. "Did you find your uncle?"

"He was at home," Fudge called back. "He was hiding."

"That's a relief. I was worried."

"What uncle?" Sheila asked.

"Uncle Feather," Fudge said. "She thinks he's my *real* uncle."

"Why would she think that?" Sheila said.

"She just does," Fudge said. "Right, Pete?"

"Yeah . . . right," I told him.

"But that doesn't make any sense," Sheila said.

"A lot of things don't make any sense," Fudge said.

Like a bird breather, I thought.

"Yoo hoo . . ." Mrs. A called again. "Come up and have a snack. Mitzi's here."

Fudge took off and Sheila panicked. "Wait for me, Fudgie . . ." she called. She tried to lift the bucket. But the Perfect Baby-Sitter hadn't stopped to think about how much rocks weigh.

"Want some help?" I asked.

"I don't need your help!" She dumped all the rocks out of the bucket, then turned it upside down over them.

"Worried someone's going to steal your rocks?" I said.

"These rocks are special."

"Oh . . . I guess I didn't notice since there's about two zillion more exactly like them."

"You're hopeless, Peter . . . really hopeless!"

"That's better than what you are!" I called. But I don't think she heard me. She was already running up the beach after Fudge.

I followed. Not that I wasn't perfectly happy on my own. But why miss out on one of Mrs. A's snacks?

The Best News
of the Century

Mitzi was smaller than Fudge, with long hair tied in a ponytail. She wore a baseball glove on her left hand. Mrs. A introduced us to her as soon as we got to the house.

"This is Fudge Feather," she said. "And this is his big brother . . ." She put her finger to her mouth and paused.

"Peter," I said, helping her out. I don't know why people can always remember Fudge's name but not mine.

"Yes," Mrs. A said. "Peter Feather."

"Feather is a funny name," Mitzi said.

"Actually, it's Hatcher," I told her, setting the record straight.

"But I thought your uncle's name is *Feather*," Mrs. A said.

"It is," Fudge told her.

"His *first* name is Feather," I explained, before things got any more confused. "*Feather* Hatcher. *Uncle* Feather Hatcher."

"Oh . . ." Mrs. A said, laughing. "I get it now. So you're the *Hatcher* boys . . . not the *Feather* boys."

"That's right," I told her.

"I like *Feather* better," Mitzi said. "And Fudge isn't a name . . . it's a candy."

"It's a name too," Fudge told her. "Right, Pete?"

"That's right," I said.

"Doesn't he have another name?" Mitzi asked me. "A *real* name?"

"It's Farley," Fudge said. He stuck out his chin, daring her to say anything more.

"Farley?" Mitzi said, opening her eyes really wide. "That's a *real* name?"

"Yes!" Fudge said.

"Grandma . . ." Mitzi said, "is Farley a name?"

"It's a beautiful name," Mrs. A said. "There

was once a handsome movie star named Farley Granger . . ." She closed her eyes and kind of sighed. Then she went into the house to get us a snack. Sheila went with her.

As soon as they were gone Mitzi got shy. She looked at the floor of the porch. Then she looked at the ceiling. She socked her fist into her baseball glove to make the pocket deeper. But she didn't say a word.

Fudge watched her and hummed a little tune. He didn't have anything to say either.

I decided it was up to me to get things going between them. So I said, "That's a good-looking baseball glove."

"I call it my *mitt-sy*," she said, hugging it to her chest. "Big gave it to me."

"Who's Big?" Fudge asked.

"My grandpa," Mitzi said. "Big Apfel."

"Big who?" I asked, sure I'd misunderstood her.

"Big Apfel," she said again.

I couldn't believe this! I kneeled beside her and spoke very slowly. "Are you telling us your grandfather is *Big Apfel*, the baseball player?"

Mitzi nodded.

"I have his baseball card," I said. "I know his stats by heart!"

"You want to play in his game?" Mitzi asked.

"His game?" I said.

She nodded again. "We play every Sunday."

"Are you saying that anyone who wants to play ball with Big Apfel, can?"

"You have to pass the over–under test first."

"What's the over–under test?"

"You have to be *over* four and *under* a hundred and four."

"And that's it?" I asked.

"That's it," she said.

"*Ya-hoo* . . ." I yelled, jumping so high I almost knocked over one of Mrs. A's hanging plants. "This is the best news I've heard in a long time!"

"Is it the best news of the century?" Fudge asked.

"It could be!" I told him, as I *ya-hooed* again.

In a minute all three of us were jumping up and down and *ya-hooing* all over the porch.

That's when the Perfect Baby-Sitter appeared, holding a pitcher of juice. "I'm gone for five minutes," she said. "Five minutes and look at you . . . carrying on like a bunch of monkeys!"

"But, honey," Fudge said, "it's the best news of the century!"

"*What's* the best news of the century?" Sheila asked.

"Who knows?" Fudge said. "I don't even know what a century is!"

I ran all the way home. As soon as I got there I called Jimmy Fargo. I'm not supposed to make long-distance calls without permission. But this was definitely a special occasion.

I was still trying to catch my breath when Jimmy answered. "Are you sitting or standing?" I asked.

"Standing."

"Well, sit down."

"Okay . . ." he said. "I'm sitting."

"Where?" I asked.

"What's the difference?"

"I want to imagine how you look when I tell you the news."

"I'm sitting on the floor in the kitchen," Jimmy said. "With my back against the refrigerator."

"Okay . . . I've got the picture."

"So what's the story?" Jimmy asked.

"You're never going to believe who our neighbor is up here." I paused for a second and took a deep breath. Then I dropped the news. "Big Apfel."

Jimmy didn't say anything.

"You fainted, right?" I said.

"No."

"But you're speechless . . ."

"No."

"You don't believe me?"

"I believe you," Jimmy said. "But I don't get

it. Did you say Big Apple is your neighbor or what?"

"I said *Big Apfel!* Boston Red Sox. The greatest center fielder of all time."

"Ty Cobb was the greatest center fielder of all time . . . or maybe Willie Mays."

I wasn't going to argue with Jimmy. Instead, I explained that this was a chance for us to play ball with *one* of the greats. I reminded him to bring his glove and his Mets cap to Maine. Then I waited for him to say something. When he didn't I asked, "Are you still there?"

"I strike out a lot," he finally said.

"Who doesn't?"

"Probably Big Apfel."

"We're not talking about the major leagues. We're talking about your basic Sunday ball game."

"Speaking of basic . . ." Jimmy said, "how's it going with the Queen of Cooties?"

"Uh . . . I hardly ever see her. She's got a job, baby-sitting."

"That's a relief!" Jimmy said.

I didn't tell him *who* she was baby-sitting.

I couldn't get to sleep that night. I kept thinking about Jimmy and me playing ball on Big Apfel's team. But that reminded me that Jimmy still doesn't know we're sharing a house with the

Tubmans. I have to come up with a good excuse—and soon—or I'll never hear the end of it from him.

I tossed and turned, as Fudge babbled in his sleep. I gave him a kick and he rolled over. After a while, I got out of bed and tiptoed down the hall to the bathroom. It's so quiet in the country . . . and dark. In the city it's never dark. You can always look out your window and see lights. It's never quiet either. You can hear the buzz of traffic even in the middle of the night.

I used the toilet, then flushed. And that's when it came to me . . . the perfect excuse for sharing a house with the Tubmans!

I flushed again and imagined myself telling Jimmy the long, sad story. I'd say: *See . . . when we first got to Maine we moved into this big, old house. It had seven bedrooms and four bathrooms and you could see the ocean from every window. But unfortunately, there was a big problem.*

What problem? Jimmy would ask.

Poison gas, I'd say. *Poison gas in all the toilets. Green, steamy, gurgling stuff that bubbled up every time we flushed.*

Blechhh . . . Jimmy would say, making a terrible face.

Dad had to call the Health Inspector, I'd continue. *She took one look and went nuts!* "This is a disaster!" *she cried.* "This is a serious environmental disaster!"

So then what? Jimmy would ask, biting his nails.

She condemned the place. Even though she was sorry about ruining our vacation, she had no choice. The police came and boarded up the house. They nailed a sign to the front door:

WARNING! POISON GAS IN TOILETS.
FLUSH AT YOUR OWN RISK!!!

Wow! Jimmy would say. *You're lucky you got out alive!*

And I'd say: *Yeah . . . I know.*

A brilliant story! I told myself as I turned out the bathroom light. Jimmy's very big on environmental issues. He's got posters all over his room—*Save the Whales, Save the Dolphins, Save the Rain Forest.* So he'll understand that the Tubmans were just trying to *Save Our Vacation* when they let us share their house.

I went back to my room and got into bed. This time I had no trouble falling asleep.

Fudge-a-mania

"How come you're in such a bad mood?" Sheila asked me the next morning.

"It must be the weather," I grumbled. Actually, it had nothing to do with the weather, which was as gray and damp as usual. It had to do with my brilliant idea from last night. Somehow, when I woke up this morning my poison-gas story sounded really weird. I wasn't sure Jimmy would buy it. And where would that leave me?

After breakfast I went back to bed. Dad says falling asleep when your body's not tired is a way of avoiding your problems. Maybe he's right. Because when I woke up, an hour later, I still didn't know what to do about Jimmy. I looked out the window. The sun was making an effort to break through the clouds. *Maybe I shouldn't worry yet*, I thought. *A lot can happen in a week. The Tubmans might decide they've had enough of Maine. They might be gone by the time Jimmy gets here.*

I got out my baseball cards and went down to the porch. I was laying them out alphabetically, by players' last names, when Mitzi showed up. I still can't believe Mitzi's grandfather is Big Apfel. I wonder why Mrs. A didn't tell us about him? Unless she's sick of people falling all over themselves when they find out who he is. I suppose I'd feel the same way if Dad were famous.

Mitzi looked at my baseball cards. "That used to be Grandpa!" she said when she spotted Big.

"What do you mean, *used to be?*" I asked. "He's still your grandpa, isn't he?"

"Yes . . . but he's different now. He has more fat."

"He was probably a lot younger when they took this picture," I said, holding up his card.

She nodded. "Where's Fudge?"

"He's planting a garden with his baby-sitter."

"Where's the garden?"

"Behind the house."

"Will you take me?"

I started to tell her to go by herself. After all, she'd walked all the way to our house on her own. But she looked at me with these big eyes. "Sometimes monsters live behind houses," she said. "And I didn't bring my monster spray."

"Monster spray?" I said.

"Grandma makes it for me. It's a secret formula. When you spray the monsters, they melt."

"Sounds like an interesting product." *Dad would have a field day with it*, I thought. He's in advertising. Commercials are his business. I can see it now:

Mitzi's Monster Spray
Made from a Grandmother's Secret Formula
Spray Twice a Day and Melt Your Monsters Away!

Mitzi held out her hand. "Will you walk me around the house?"

How could I refuse? I walked her to the backyard, where Sheila and Fudge were hard at work. They'd already dug out a plot of land. Now they were lining up rows of pink rocks from the beach. "You're planting rocks?" I asked.

"Yes," Fudge said. "Rocks don't need sun or water. They don't get slugs. Animals can't eat them. And they never die."

I looked at Sheila.

"It was *his* idea," she said.

"It was *my* idea," Fudge repeated.

"I like this garden," Mitzi said. She got down on her hands and knees to help.

"Mom and Dad are going to be surprised when they see your garden," I told Fudge.

"I know," he said.

"They're going to be surprised that you dug up this much grass to plant rocks. Especially since this backyard doesn't belong to us."

"Who does it belong to?" Fudge asked.

"The people who own this house," I told him.

"So . . ." he said, "the people who own this house will be happy when they see my garden."

"Maybe," I told him. "Or maybe they'll say, *Who dug up our backyard?*"

"Really, Peter," Sheila said. "You're such a worrier!"

"Yeah, Pete," Fudge said. "You worry too much."

"I don't worry!" I told them. "I think ahead."

When the rocks were all planted—six rows of them, with ten in each row—Mitzi scooped up a handful of dirt. "Now let's make mud pie!"

"Mud pie," Fudge said. "That's what they have for dessert at Tico-Taco. Right, Pete?"

"But it's not made of mud," I told him.

"Then why do they call it *mud pie?*" he asked.

"Because it looks like mud," I explained.

"Yum . . . mud pie," Mitzi said, licking the dirt off her fingers.

"Spit that out right now!" Sheila told her. "That's full of bacteria."

"Yum . . . bacteria!" Mitzi said. "I love bacteria. Don't you, Fudge?"

"Bacteria's my favorite," Fudge said. Then he looked up at me. "What's *bacteria*, Pete?"

"They're like germs," I told him.

"Yum . . . germs!" Mitzi said. "Germs are really tasty."

"Cooties are tasty, too," Fudge said. "And slugs. Slugs are fat and juicy!"

"You two are disgusting!" Sheila said.

"*Germy germy germs* and *sluggy sluggy slugs,*" Mitzi sang.

"*Yummy yummy down my tummy!*" Fudge held his arms straight out to the sides and began to twirl. Mitzi copied him. They twirled around and around—faster and faster—until they got so dizzy they fell to the ground, screaming and laughing. Then they started all over again.

"Stop that!" Sheila shouted.

"We can't," Fudge yelled, twirling and whirling.

"It's *Fudge-a-mania!*" Mitzi shrieked. "Once you get it you can never stop."

"I'm going to count to three . . ." Sheila shouted.

But Sheila's threat didn't bother them. "You better watch out," Fudge sang, "because it's catching!" He twirled over to me and swatted my behind. "Now you've got it, Pete! You've got *Fudge-a-mania* too!"

I started twirling, slowly at first—then faster and faster—until everything was a blur. I twirled over to Sheila and smacked her on the back. "Look out, Sheila . . . you just caught it from me!"

"I did not catch anything from you!" Sheila shouted. "I will never catch anything from you!"

The door to the house slammed and out marched Libby. She was wearing her Snoopy T-shirt. It's so big it hangs down to her knees. She stomped across the yard. "Just what exactly is going on here?" she asked. She didn't wait for an answer. "And how am I supposed to sleep with this racket?"

"Sleep?" Mitzi asked. "Now?"

"Yes, now!" Libby said. "It's only ten o'clock in the morning!"

"You sleep until ten o'clock in the morning?" Mitzi said, like she couldn't believe it.

Libby put her hands on her hips and glared. "I try!"

"But morning is the best time to play," Mitzi said.

"Who is this kid?" Libby asked Sheila.

"Mitzi Apfel," Sheila said. "A neighbor."

"I'm five," Mitzi told her. "And I walked here all by myself. I didn't need anyone to show me the way."

"I'll tell you what *you* need . . ." Libby began.

But Mitzi didn't wait to hear what Libby had to say. She raced off, shouting, "It's *Fudge-a-mania!*"

Fudge followed Mitzi.

Sheila chased both of them.

"You're all *maniacs!*" Libby shouted.

"*Fudge-a-maniacs,*" I added.

Either Libby didn't get my joke or she decided to ignore it. Because she said, "This is all your fault, Peter! Chaos follows you and your family."

"Chaos," I said. "I don't believe I know him."

That got Libby really mad. "*Chaos,*" she yelled, "*a state of utter confusion or disorder!*" Then she stomped back to the house and went inside, letting the screen door slam behind her. I couldn't help laughing.

When Mom and Dad saw Fudge's garden, I expected them to really let him have it! They've always taught us to respect other people's property. But when Fudge explained his reasons for planting rocks Mom said, "That's very good thinking."

"A good baby-sitter encourages creative thinking," Sheila said.

"But doesn't this show a lack of respect for other people's property?" I asked.

"Well . . ." Mom said, "it would have been better if Fudge had checked with us before he started. But his idea was so well-thought-out. Rocks don't need sun or water, animals can't eat them . . ."

"Yeah . . . yeah . . ." I said. "I've heard all about it."

Grandma wandered across the yard with Buzzy Senior. She took one look at Fudge's garden and said, "Isn't my grandson an original, Buzzy?"

"Actually, it was mostly *my* idea!" Sheila said.

"That's not what you said this morning!" I shouted at Sheila. "This morning you said it was *his* idea."

"Just shut your face for once, Peter Hatcher!" she shouted back.

"Who's going to make me?" I yelled.

"Children . . ." Grandma said. "Let's be kind."

"*Kind* is a word your grandson doesn't know, Muriel!" Sheila shouted.

"He knows it," Grandma said. "But sometimes he forgets what it means."

"And *she* doesn't?" I asked.

"Sometimes she forgets, too," Grandma admitted.

"I don't see why you two can't get along as well as your dogs," Buzzy Senior said.

I looked toward the house. Turtle and Jake were playing together. You'd think Turtle would show more loyalty. You'd think he'd understand about Sheila and me.

Tootsie grabbed my leg. "Up, Pee . . . up . . ."

"Not now!" I said.

"Now . . . now . . . now . . ."

But I wasn't in the mood for baby tricks. So I shook her off and she fell over on her backside. It took a few seconds for her to react. Then she scrunched up her face—her mouth started twitching—her breath came fast. She made her little hands into fists, shut her eyes tight and opened her mouth. WAAAAAAAAAAHHHH!!! Once she got going, you could hear her a mile away.

"What happened, Tootsie Pie?" Dad asked, as he lifted her into his arms.

Tootsie kept screaming and Mom looked at me. "Was that necessary, Peter?"

"Was what necessary?" I said.

Mom just shook her head.

"You see how much trouble you cause for everyone?" Sheila shouted at me.

How come I'm getting blamed for this? I thought.
All I did was ask one simple question.

Fudge held his arms out to Mom. "Up . . ." he
said. "Up . . . up . . . up . . ."

"You want to play *baby?*" Mom asked.

"Goo goo gaa gaa," Fudge said, jumping into
Mom's arms.

"You're getting heavy," Mom said, planting a
kiss on his head.

"But not too heavy for my mommy . . .
right?"

I shook my head, then turned away and
watched Dad, galloping around the yard with
Tootsie on his shoulders. In a minute Tootsie
was laughing. I remember when Dad carried
Fudge that way. And there's a photo of me on
his shoulders, too. I'm laughing really hard
and grabbing Dad's hair. He had a lot more to
grab then.

"Go, horsey . . ." Tootsie called, as Dad
galloped in the other direction.

Being a baby is so easy, I thought. *Riding around
on Dad's shoulders, knowing he'd never let you fall.
And doing and saying whatever you please, without
worrying about what the other guy will think.*

Grandma put her arm around my shoulder.
"It's not easy being the firstborn, is it?"

I looked at her and smiled. She knew exactly
what I was feeling.

Dizzy from Izzy

I hung out at the beach almost all day on Friday, hoping to catch a glimpse of Big Apfel. I guess Mrs. A finally noticed because she came out on her porch and said, "If you're looking for Fudge he's down at the tide pool with Mitzi and Sheila."

"I'm not looking for him," I explained. "I . . . uh . . . just wanted to ask Big a question about the game."

As soon as I said *Big* I wondered if I should have called him *Mr.* Apfel instead.

But Mrs. A acted as if it was okay. She said,

"Big's on a fishing trip. He'll be back in a few days."

A few days! "What about the game on Sunday?" I asked.

"There's no game this Sunday," Mrs. A said. "It's the annual antique show. They set it up on the high school field."

"Antique show?"

"Yes," Mrs. A said. "And Big gets so upset about the game being canceled, he has to leave town. But don't worry . . . he'll be back before next Sunday. Big never misses a ball game."

I guess Mrs. A could tell how disappointed I was because she said, "I just baked chocolate chip cookies . . ."

"No, thank you," I said. "I'm not very hungry."

I ran home and announced the bad news. "No ball game this Sunday because of some dumb antique show!"

"I read about that in the local paper," Mom said. "I think we should go."

"Forget it," I told her. "You're not getting me anywhere near those stupid antiques!"

"It's good there's no game," Fudge said, "because I *still* don't have a *mitt-sy.*" He looked at Dad. He's been begging for a *mitt-sy* ever since Mitzi showed him hers, two days ago.

"Tomorrow afternoon," Dad told him.

"Promise?" Fudge asked.

"Promise," Dad said.

When Mitzi came over the next morning, Fudge said, "I'm getting my *mitt-sy* this afternoon."

"That's nice," Mitzi said. But she was more interested in the book she was carrying than in Fudge's baseball glove. "Did you know I can read?" she asked.

"So can I," Fudge said.

Mitzi held up her book and pointed to the title. "What does this say?"

"I can't read everything," Fudge said. "I can read *Hop on Pop* and dinosaur books."

I don't know if he can really read *Hop on Pop* or if he's memorized it. But it's true that he knows all the words.

"The name of this book is *Tell Me a Mitzi,*" she said, smiling.

"Is it, Pete?" Fudge asked.

"That's what it says," I told him.

Fudge looked surprised.

Mitzi opened the book. "And it's all about me and my baby brother, Jacob."

"You don't have a baby brother," Fudge said.

"I do so. And his name is Jacob."

"Where is he?"

"In Boston with Mommy and Daddy. He's not old enough to visit Grandma and Big by himself. He can't even talk. And he makes poop in his diaper."

"So does Tootsie," Fudge said.

"I hold my nose when Jacob gets changed," Mitzi said.

"I hold my nose when Tootsie gets changed," Fudge said.

"One time Jacob got into his diaper and played with his poop," Mitzi said. "Ooohhhh . . . it was so bad!"

"This conversation is getting pretty bad!" I told them.

They looked at each other and laughed.

"Let me see that book," Fudge said.

Mitzi handed it to him and he flipped through the pages. "How come it's about you?"

"Because I'm special," Mitzi said.

That afternoon I went to town with Dad and Fudge. The sports store had only one baseball glove small enough to fit him but he didn't mind. "Now I have my own *mitt-sy*," he told the clerk.

"Yes," the clerk said. "I guess you do. And if you put a few drops of oil on it every day you'll make it nice and soft."

"A few drops of oil," Fudge repeated, as we left the store. He was wearing his glove and kept punching his fist into it the way Mitzi had with hers.

When Dad told us he had to stop off at Sawyer's Market, Fudge asked if he could go to the library.

"Sure," Dad said.

The library is next door to Sawyer's. From the outside it looks like a little house. There are pots of flowers on the steps and even a screen door. But inside it's like a regular library. I left Fudge in the children's room and headed for the sports section. There were a lot of books about baseball. I was browsing through one that looked interesting when Fudge tugged at my shirt. "I can't find it," he said.

"Find what?"

"The book I want."

I figured he was looking for something like *Your Favorite Brontosaurus* or *The Last Tyrannosaurus Rex*. So I said, "Go ask the librarian."

"You come, too."

"I'm busy."

"Please, Pete! This is important."

"Oh . . . all right." I walked him to the checkout desk. The regular librarian wasn't there. Instead, there was a girl, maybe sixteen or seventeen. She wore a pin on her shirt that said

Library Assistant. She was reading a book. It must have been really good because she didn't even notice we were standing in front of her until Fudge spoke. "Do you have *Tell Me a Fudge?*" he asked.

I almost fell through the floor.

"Pardon?" the girl said, looking up at us. Her eyes were a deep, dark brown—like the best chocolate.

"*Tell Me a Fudge,*" he repeated. "That's the book I want."

"It doesn't sound familiar," she said.

"It could be called *Tell Me a Farley,*" Fudge said.

I coughed twice but she didn't even glance my way. "Did you look it up in the card catalog?" she asked Fudge.

"No," Fudge said.

"Well, let's give it a try. Our computer's down today." She marked her place in the book she was reading. When she closed it I tried to read the title upside down. I think it was called *Beginner's Love* but I'm not sure.

Fudge followed her to the card catalog and I followed Fudge. "What's your name?" he asked.

"Isobel," she said. "But my friends call me Izzy."

"Izzy . . ." he said. "I like that."

"What's yours?" she asked him.

"Farley," he said. "But my friends call me Fudge."

"Oh . . ." Isobel said. "What an interesting name." She thumbed through the cards in the *T* drawer. "We have *Tell Me a Mitzi* and *Tell Me a Trudy*. But I don't see *Tell Me a Fudge* or *Tell Me a Farley*."

"It has to be there," Fudge said.

Isobel went through the cards again. "Nope . . . I'm sorry."

Fudge scrunched up his face and his breath came fast. *Oh no!* I thought. *He wouldn't . . . not here . . . not now . . .*

But I was wrong. "It's not fair!" he cried, throwing himself on the floor. Then he kicked and he banged his fists and he screamed. *"It's not fair!!!"*

Isobel looked at me. I wanted to disappear. Lucky for us, there were only a few other people in the library. One woman came over to see what was happening, but she wasn't impressed. She shook her head, then went back to the stacks, where she'd been browsing. A man stuck his head out of a reading room and called, "Quiet, please . . . this is a library!"

But Fudge kept on kicking *and* screaming *and* banging his fists.

"Stop!" I hissed. "You're making a scene."

"I can't help it," he cried.

"You're too old for this."

"I'm not too old. I'm only five."

I would have walked out and left him there, except for Isobel. She kneeled beside him. "Fudge . . ." she said, very softly.

Fudge looked at her. His face was blotchy red and his nose was runny.

"Who knows more about a Fudge or a Farley than you?"

"Nobody . . ."

"Exactly," she said. "So maybe you should write this book yourself."

"I can't write," Fudge said. "My fingers hurt from just printing my name."

"Maybe you can tell the stories to someone else . . . like your brother . . . and he'll write them down for you." Isobel smiled at me as if we were sharing some secret. I think I smiled back but I'm not sure. I felt like I was in a dream and everything was happening in slow motion.

Fudge sat up. "I'll think about it," he said. Isobel handed him a tissue from her pocket. But he doesn't know how to blow his nose. So he just wiped the whole mess across his face. Then he stood, took Isobel's hand and walked back to the check-out desk with her.

"That's a nice-looking baseball glove," she told him.

"I call it my *mitt-sy*," Fudge said. "And I'm going

to oil it every day . . . to keep it nice and soft."

I wondered if Isobel oiled her skin. I wondered if it felt as soft as it looked. My mind drifted off . . . I pictured myself on a desert island with Isobel. *It doesn't matter that I'm years older than you, Peter,* she was saying, *because you're so mature for your age . . .*

Fudge tugged at my hand. "Pete . . ."

"What?"

"I'll go tell Dad we're done, okay?"

I nodded.

As soon as Fudge was gone Isobel said, "Did you want to check that out?" When I didn't answer she reached for the book I was holding. "Do you have your card?" she asked.

"My card?"

"Yes . . . your library card."

"No . . . I guess I forgot it."

"That's okay . . . I can hold the book for you until next Saturday."

"Next Saturday," I said.

I don't know how I got out of there, my legs were shaking so bad. I was feeling kind of weak all over and dizzy, too.

Fudge came out of Sawyer's Market just as I came out of the library. "Dad says he's next on line. He'll meet us back at the car." He stopped for a minute and looked at me. "What's wrong, Pete?"

"Nothing . . . why?"

"You look weird. Are you going to puke?"

"No . . . I'm just a little . . . dizzy."

"Put your head down," he said. "That's what Mom always tells me when I'm dizzy."

"I'm not that kind of dizzy," I said.

"Oh."

"It's more like I'm floating." I started to sing, *"Who can explain it, who can tell you why?"*

That night when I got into bed, I stared into my Kreskin's Crystal and repeated Isobel's name over and over. I didn't care that her friends called her Izzy. To me she'd always be Isobel. A beautiful name. A name that really fits her. If I were the Amazing Kreskin I'd be able to plan all my dreams. I'd probably be able to transfer thoughts from my head into Isobel's and make her dream about me. I closed my eyes and concentrated. *Isobel . . . Isobel . . .*

But then Fudge came racing into the room. He took a flying leap and landed on my bed. I hid my Kreskin's Crystal under my pillow where he couldn't get his hands on it.

"I'm ready to start my book," he announced. "I'll say it and you write it down."

"Why don't you wait until tomorrow? Then your baby-sitter can write it down for you."

"I can't wait, Pete."

"Why not?"

"*Who can explain it, who can tell you why?*" He laughed as he handed me paper and a pencil.

There was no way he was going to give up. The sooner I started writing, the sooner I'd be able to get back to Isobel. So I took the pencil and said, "Okay . . . let's go."

"*Tell Me a Fudge,*" he said, "*by Farley Drexel Hatcher. Chapter One—How Turtle Got His Name.*"

He waited while I wrote that down. Then he yawned. "That's it for tonight, Pete. Tomorrow I'll write Chapter Two."

"I can hardly wait," I told him.

He got into his own bed and two seconds later he was out cold.

I took my Kreskin's Crystal from under my pillow and held it tightly. *Isobel . . . Isobel . . . Tell Me an Isobel . . .*

I had a dream that night, but it wasn't about Isobel. It was about Sheila Tubman! I woke up feeling really disappointed.

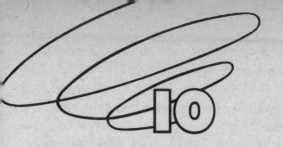

Green Gurgling Gas

On Wednesday Sheila got a phone call during breakfast. As soon as she hung up she started bawling.

"What's wrong, honey?" Fudge asked.

"My friend Mouse Ellis has chicken pox and can't come to Maine!"

Grandma put her arms around Sheila. "You must be terribly disappointed."

"I am," Sheila wailed. "Everything happens to me! Why does it have to be *my* friend who gets sick? Why couldn't Jimmy Fargo get chicken pox instead?"

"Jimmy had chicken pox in second grade," I said. "Don't you remember . . . we all had them."

That made Sheila cry even harder. "But it's soooo unfair!"

"Where is it written that life is fair?" Grandma asked. "It's all ups and downs, isn't it, Buzzy?"

Buzzy Senior nodded. "These things happen," he told Sheila.

That's when I burped. I didn't mean to. It just came out. Probably I drank my orange juice too fast. But Sheila glared at me. "I heard that, Peter!"

"Heard what?" I asked.

"That stupid laugh!" Sheila said.

"That was no laugh. That was a burp."

Sheila turned to Buzzy Senior. "Grandpa . . . make him stop! He's so mean . . . he's glad Mouse can't come to Maine."

Before I had the chance to explain, Tootsie flicked a spoonful of oatmeal across the table. It landed on Sheila's face, halfway between her mouth and her eyes.

"You see . . ." Sheila cried. "You see how everything happens to me?"

"It's just oatmeal," Grandma said, handing Sheila a piece of paper towel.

"That's not the point!" Sheila turned and ran from the room.

I sure hoped things would improve before tonight, when Jimmy Fargo gets here!

After breakfast, Mom helped get my room ready for Jimmy. She moved Fudge's things down the hall, into the room Grandma is sharing with Tootsie. She set up a rollaway bed for Fudge right next to Tootsie's crib. "I hate crowding you in like this," Mom said to Grandma.

"I don't mind," Grandma said. "Sleeping in the same room as my grandchildren is a privilege. It's a lot more fun than sleeping in a room by myself."

"You should get married, Grandma," Fudge said. "Then you wouldn't have to sleep in a room by yourself." He jumped on the rollaway bed.

"That bed isn't designed for jumping," Mom told him. "It's going to collapse if you don't stop."

Fudge tumbled off the bed like some Olympic gymnast and landed on his feet. If I tried that I'd probably break a leg. "Do you still snore, Grandma?" he asked.

"Fudgie!" Mom said. "That's not a polite question."

But Grandma didn't mind. She said, "I really don't know, Fudge. You'll have to tell me."

"Snoring keeps the monsters away," he said.

"Yes," Grandma said, "I'm sure it does."

"When I get married I won't have monsters in my room," Fudge said.

"Says who?" I asked.

"You don't get monsters when you sleep in a bed with somebody else."

"That's why you want to get married?" I said. "So you won't get monsters in your room?"

"Why else would I get married?"

"You should talk to Mitzi," I told him. "She's got monster spray."

"Monster spray?"

"Mitzi's Monster Spray," I said in a deep voice, trying out my commercial. *"Made from a grandmother's secret formula. Spray twice a day and melt your monsters away!"*

"Really, Peter . . ." Mom said.

But Fudge liked the idea. He jumped back onto the rollaway bed and bounced up and down singing, "Monster spray melts your monsters away!"

"Fudgie . . ." Mom warned. But it was too late. Both ends of the rollaway bed sprang up, catching Fudge in the middle.

I imagined the headline in tonight's paper:

FIVE-YEAR-OLD FLATTENED BY ROLLAWAY BED

"Get me out of here!" Fudge yelled.

"Okay . . . okay . . ." Mom and Grandma held the bed apart and I pulled him out.

"Stupid . . . stupid . . . bed!" Fudge cried, kicking it. "If you do that to me again I'm going to chop you up in little pieces!"

"Let's not blame the bed," Mom said.

Later, when we were out in the backyard, Fudge told Buzzy Senior what had happened.

"Those beds can be very tricky," Buzzy Senior said.

Fudge nodded. Then, out of nowhere, he said, "Do you snore, Buzzy?"

"I used to snore," Buzzy Senior said, as if Fudge's question were perfectly natural. "But since I sleep alone now I really don't know."

"How come you sleep alone?"

"Because my wife died."

Fudge got this serious look on his face. You could tell he was thinking hard. But after a minute his face lit up and he said, "You should sleep with Grandma!"

"Fudge!" Mom said.

"Well, they're best friends," Fudge told her. "Like Pete and Jimmy. And Jimmy's going to sleep in Pete's room . . . right?"

Buzzy Senior and Grandma looked at each other and laughed.

That afternoon the sky turned gray and it started to drizzle. The Tubmans decided to drive to Bar Harbor. That's the town where all the tourists go. It's got hundreds of little shops selling T-shirts with sayings about Maine, like *Cool as a Moose in Bar Harbor* or *Maine, Fifty Miles from Nowhere.*

"Count me out," Libby said. "I've got to be at work by three."

"Count me out, too," Sheila said. "The Hatchers depend on me to baby-sit Fudge."

But Mom convinced Sheila she deserved an afternoon off. If you ask me everyone was feeling sorry for the Cootie Queen just because Mouse got sick and couldn't come to Maine. Everyone but me, that is.

Still, I felt relieved when the Tubmans left. *I hope they go out for a pizza and catch a late movie,* I thought. *I hope they like the action in Bar Harbor so much they decide to stay for a week!*

They still weren't back when Mr. Fargo called from town, asking Mom for directions to the house. That was a good sign because by then it was after six.

I waited on the porch. When I saw Mr. Fargo's truck I ran down to the road. His truck is really old, with rust spots around the fenders. It's painted the color of bile. Not that I've ever seen bile but last year in school we learned about the digestive system and that's the way I imagine it. A sick greenish-brown color.

Turtle barked. "It's Jimmy," I told him, as I waved Mr. Fargo into our driveway.

At first, Jimmy couldn't get out of the truck. The door on his side wouldn't budge. He kicked it a couple of times, then banged it with his shoulder. Finally it creaked open. By then we were laughing.

Turtle jumped up and tried to lick Jimmy's face. "Good boy . . . nice doggie . . ." Jimmy said, patting him.

"Turtle knows a friend when he sees one," I said. Jimmy gave me a bear hug and we slapped hands. It was great to see him! But that didn't stop me from checking over my shoulder. I hoped the Tubmans wouldn't show up now.

Jimmy also took a look around. "You were right," he said. "You can't even see Sheila's house from here. I guess it's through those woods over there."

"Well, see . . ." I began.

But then Mom opened the front door and called to us.

Inside, Dad had a fire going in the big, stone fireplace. Fudge was stretched out on the floor with his Crayolas, illustrating Chapter One of his book. Tootsie was scooting around on her Toddle-Bike and Grandma was reading. She put down her book to greet Mr. Fargo.

Jimmy headed straight for Uncle Feather's cage. "Bonjour, stupid," he said.

"Bonjour, stupid!" Uncle Feather answered.

Jimmy laughed. "Good old Uncle Feather."

"Good old Uncle Feather . . ."

"Please, Jimmy . . ." Mom said. "Don't encourage him. Once you get him going it's hard to turn him off."

"Turn him off . . . turn him off . . ."

"You see what I mean?" Mom asked.

"See what I mean . . . see what I mean?"

I motioned for Jimmy to sneak away from Uncle Feather's cage. Jimmy got down on all fours and crawled across the living room, out of Uncle Feather's sight.

As he did, Tootsie held her arms out to Mr. Fargo. "Up . . ." she said. "Up!"

Mr. Fargo lifted her high above his head and

shook her. Tootsie loved it. She has this thing for bearded men. She'll raise her arms and say *Up* to any guy with a beard. Mom says it's because Dad used to have one. But I'm not so sure. We're going to have to teach her to be more careful. I can just see her walking down Broadway in a few years, holding out her arms to every bearded weirdo on the street.

Mom took Tootsie from Mr. Fargo. "Thanks for driving Jimmy all this way, Frank," she said. "I know what a long trip it is."

"Used to come up here in the old days," Mr. Fargo said, "with my ex-wife. You remember my *ex*-wife, don't you?"

Uh oh . . . I thought. *I hope he's not going to start in on Mrs. Fargo. Because Jimmy really hates it when he does.*

"How about something to drink, Frank?" Dad asked. I was glad he changed the subject.

"Some fizzy water, if you have it," Mr. Fargo said.

"Coming right up."

Mom smiled, but I could tell she was tense. A lot of people get tense around Mr. Fargo. I think it's because he never smiles—even when he's trying to be friendly. "How about this Maine weather?" Mom asked.

"You have to have weather, whether or not!" Mr. Fargo said.

Jimmy groaned. "That's so bad, Dad!"

I heard a car pull into the driveway. *Oh no*, I thought. *Not now!* The car doors slammed and a minute later the Tubmans came bounding up the porch steps and into the house. Sheila headed straight for the fire. "It's soooo cold and damp . . ." she began. She stopped when she saw Jimmy. "Oh . . . it's you!"

"What's *she* doing here?" Jimmy asked.

"I'll explain later," I whispered.

But Sheila explained for me. "I happen to live here! This happens to be *my* house!"

"I thought this was *your* house," Jimmy said to me.

"Well . . . uh . . . see . . ." I began.

"We share the living room and the kitchen," Sheila said. "We eat breakfast and dinner together every day."

Jimmy looked at me. "I don't get it."

"It's like two houses in one," I told him. "It's like . . . they're connected."

"Connected?" Jimmy said.

"Yeah . . . joined together," I said. I looked over at Sheila. She was enjoying this.

"Joined together?" Jimmy said.

Sheila laughed out loud. I glared at her. "See . . . our family lives over there . . ." I explained, pointing to our side of the house. "And her family lives over here . . . and the living room and kitchen are sort of in the middle."

Jimmy just stood there with his mouth half open. Sheila picked Jake up and started kissing her. "Isn't my dog adorable?" she asked Jimmy, between smooches.

"I thought you're afraid of dogs," Jimmy said.

"She is," I told him.

"That's not true!" Sheila said. "I just don't like big, *smelly* dogs."

Turtle, who was asleep in the corner, raised his head. *Attack!* I told him mentally. But he didn't get my message. He just scratched himself and went back to sleep. Sheila carried Jake over to Jimmy and put her in his arms. "Rub her belly. She loves that."

Jimmy held Jake like a baby. "She's so soft."

This was too much! I was glad when Dad called, "Dinner's almost ready. Pasta with Anne's special sauce."

Mr. Fargo suddenly came to life and said, "Better get our things inside, Jimmy."

When Jimmy and his father went out to the car, Mom said, "Did he say *our* things?"

"He meant Jimmy's things," I told her.

"I hope so," Mom said, looking worried.

But then Jimmy carried one duffel bag into the house and Mr. Fargo carried another. "I don't have much," Mr. Fargo said. "Just this and my art supplies."

"You're planning to stay with us?" Mom asked.

"No point in trying to camp out in this weather," Mr. Fargo told her.

From the look on Mom's face I thought she might faint.

There was a long, awkward silence. Finally Dad said, "You can have the sofa in here, Frank. It's the only available space left."

"Unless Grandma sleeps with Buzzy Senior," Fudge said. "Then I can sleep in Grandma's bed and Mr. Fargo can have the rollaway."

Everyone looked at Fudge, including Mr. Fargo. "Don't go to any trouble," he said. "This sofa looks mighty good to me."

Later, when Jimmy and I were in the bathroom getting ready for bed, he said, "I'm really embarrassed about my father. Anybody can see you've already got too many people in this house."

"It's no big deal." I handed him a clean towel.

"Yeah, right . . . that's how come your mother almost fainted."

"Only because we're out of beds," I said.

"You think my father cares about beds? He likes to sleep on the floor."

"It's okay. Forget it."

Jimmy spit out toothpaste. "You know he's weird. He doesn't mean to be . . . but he is."

"He's not *that* weird." I flushed the toilet, which reminded me of my poison-gas story. "Look . . ." I said, "I'm embarrassed too. I should have told you about sharing a house with the Tubmans. But I didn't find out until we got up here and then . . . well . . . I was afraid if I told you, you wouldn't come."

"I probably wouldn't have," Jimmy said. "But now that I'm here, it doesn't seem that bad."

I was glad I wouldn't have to lie to Jimmy after all. And telling him the truth wasn't as hard as I thought it would be. Still, I couldn't help wondering how he would have reacted to my story.

I decided to find out. As soon as we were in bed I said, "Did you hear about the poison gas?"

"What poison gas?"

"The poison gas in the toilets?"

"What toilets?"

"Some guy up here . . . he had poison gas in all his toilets."

"What do you mean, poison gas?" Jimmy faced me and propped himself up on his elbow.

"It was this green, steamy, gurgling stuff that bubbled up every time he flushed."

"Green . . . steamy . . . gurgling stuff . . ." Jimmy started to laugh.

"It's not funny," I said. "It's an environmental disaster!"

"An environmental disaster?" Jimmy said. "Where'd you read that . . . in the *National Enquirer?*"

"You don't think it's possible?"

"Yeah, I think it's possible . . . if the guy ate something that didn't agree with him." Jimmy broke up laughing.

"Ha ha," I said, as I reached over and turned out the light.

"Ha ha . . ." a voice repeated. And it wasn't Jimmy.

I jumped out of bed and opened the door. Fudge was sitting on the floor right outside my room. "What are you doing here?" I asked.

"I don't know."

"Didn't anybody ever tell you you're not supposed to listen to private conversations?"

"No."

I picked him up and turned him upside down. I held him that way until his face turned purple. "Put me down, Pete!"

"Not until you promise never to do that again!"

"Okay . . . I promise."

I didn't believe him for a second but I put him down anyway. "Now, go to bed!"

"I can't."

"Why not?"

"I'm afraid of the rollaway."

"The rollaway can't hurt you."

"Yes it can. It can mash me. So I'll sleep in here with you and Jimmy."

"No you won't!" I carried him down the hall and dropped him on the rollaway bed. Grandma and Tootsie were already asleep.

Fudge listened to Grandma, who was snoring softly. "No monsters tonight," he whispered, pointing in her direction.

"Right," I whispered back. "Now go to sleep."

"Tuck me in," he said.

I tucked him in.

"Now kiss me good-night."

I was about to drop a light one on his forehead when he reached up, grabbed me around the neck and pulled me down. Then he planted a big, wet smackeroo right in the middle of my face. "Sweet dreams, Pete!"

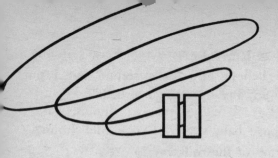

The I.S.A.F. Club

Fudge was counting his Cheerios when Jimmy and I came down to breakfast the next day. As soon as we sat down Sheila waltzed in, wearing her fuzzy pink robe and her bunny slippers, as usual. Jimmy took one look and doubled over. Sheila poured herself a glass of juice, then made herself comfortable at the table between Buzzy Senior and Fudge. "Good morning, sweetheart," Buzzy Senior said, kissing her cheek.

"Good morning, honey," Fudge said, kissing her other cheek.

"What is this . . . Camp Kissy Face?" Jimmy asked.

"You wish!" Sheila said.

"Oh yeah . . . I really wish . . ." Jimmy said.

"Sheila's my baby-sitter," Fudge told Jimmy. "But maybe she's going to be my wife, too."

"Wife?" Jimmy said to Sheila.

"*Maybe*," Sheila said. "Nothing's definite yet."

"It all depends on Mitzi," Fudge said.

"Mitzi?" Jimmy asked.

"She's my friend. She has monster spray. She's trying to get some for me. Then I won't have to get married."

Jimmy gave me a look, then sliced a banana into his cornflakes.

"Buzzy Senior and Grandma are best friends," Fudge continued. "But they don't sleep in the same room."

"Why don't you save the morning report till after breakfast?" I said.

"I can't." He nibbled on his Cheerios, eating one little circle at a time. "I might forget."

"Pass the milk, please," Jimmy said. Grandma passed it to him and Jimmy poured some over his cereal.

"Jake will roll over if you give her cheddar cheese," Fudge said, still going strong. "But if you give Tootsie cheese she spits it out."

"Okay . . ." I said, "that's it! Jimmy doesn't want to hear any more. Jimmy wants to have his breakfast in peace."

"Wait!" Fudge shouted. "I'm not finished!"

"Oh, yes you are!" I told him.

But did he listen? *Does he ever listen?*

"Libby works at Ickle's Ice Cream Parlor," he blabbed. "She puts extra sprinkles on my cone. Annnnnd . . ." He stretched out the word, making sure he had everyone's attention. "Pete got dizzy from Izzy at the library."

That did it! I reached across the table and grabbed him by his sweatshirt. "One more word and I'm going to let you have it!"

"Okay . . ." He went back to counting his Cheerios.

"What was that about Peter getting dizzy?" Sheila asked.

"That was a joke!" I told her.

"He felt like he was floating," Fudge said.

I shoved back my chair and raced around the table, ready to destroy him.

"Grandma . . ." Fudge cried. "Heeelp . . . !"

Grandma shouted, *"Enough!"*

"Eeee . . ." Tootsie shrieked. "Eeee . . . eee . . . eeee . . ."

This time Grandma stood up and banged a wooden spoon against a pot. We all quieted down and ate our breakfasts, not that I was hungry anymore.

When we finished, we helped Grandma clean up. Then Sheila danced across the living room in her bunny slippers, singing, "*He got dizzy from Izzy at the library . . .*"

Mr. Fargo, who'd been sleeping on the couch, suddenly sat up. He looked confused. "Where am I?" he asked.

"You're in Maine, Dad," Jimmy told him. "Remember? You're sleeping on the sofa in the Hatchers' living room."

"You mean the *Tubmans'* living room," Sheila said, as she danced out the door onto the porch. Jimmy followed her and I followed Jimmy. No way was I going to leave the two of them alone.

It was a warm, sunny morning, for a change. Everything smelled fresh and clean from last night's rain. Too bad Sheila had to spoil it with her musical act. She danced from one end of the porch to the other, singing. "*Dizzy from Izzy . . . la dee dah . . . maybe it's love . . . la dee dah . . .*"

"It has nothing to do with love!" I told Jimmy. "Fudge made the whole thing up!"

"Dizzy . . ." Sheila said, "floating? Sounds like love to me."

"Yeah, Peter," Jimmy said. "Sounds like love to me, too."

"I've seen Izzy," Sheila told Jimmy. "She's got curly hair and a fat behind."

"It's not fat!" I shouted.

"If it's not fat how come it wiggles when she walks?" Sheila asked, parading across the porch. She tried to imitate Isobel but wound up waddling like a duck instead.

"So when do I get to meet this Izzy?" Jimmy asked.

"I have an idea," Sheila said. "We can ride our bikes to the library this morning."

"I thought you have a job," I said. "I thought you have to baby-sit Fudge."

"Haven't you heard?" Sheila asked. "Fudge is invited to Mitzi's. All I have to do is walk him over and I'm free."

"I hope my mother's not paying you for that!"

"Business between your mother and me is private," Sheila said.

Then Jimmy said, "I didn't bring a bike."

"No problem," Sheila told him. "We have extras in the garage."

"Jimmy's here to visit *me!*" I told Sheila. "And *I'll* decide what we're going to do." I went back inside, slamming the door as I did.

First he tells me he can't stand Sheila. Next thing you know it's like they're best friends. Who needs this?

I went up to my room, kicked yesterday's

clothes out of the way, and sat on the edge of my bed.

In a minute Jimmy joined me. He sat on the edge of his bed. "Sorry," he said. "I don't know what got into me. There's plenty of reasons for feeling dizzy besides love."

I didn't say anything.

"You're not mad, are you?" Jimmy asked.

"Why should I be mad?"

"Then you don't mind if we ride into town?"

"Why would I mind? I was just trying to help you out since I know you can't stand being around the Cootie Queen."

"Yeah . . . but I feel kind of sorry for her, since her friend got chicken pox and all."

"She told you about Mouse?"

"Yeah. And I know how disappointed you'd be if I'd come down with chicken pox."

"You had them in second grade."

"I know, but just suppose . . ."

Dad adjusted the seat on one of the extra bikes for Jimmy. Then he handed him a bike helmet. "Safety first," he said. "The road to town is very busy."

"We'll be careful," Sheila promised. "I took a course in bicycle safety so I know all the rules."

"What don't you know?" I muttered.

"I don't know how to turn perfect cart-wheels," Sheila said. "But with Muriel's help I'm improving."

I jumped on my bike and rode away from the house, leaving Jimmy and Sheila behind. At the end of the dirt road I turned right and pedaled as fast as I could. I pedaled harder and faster than I ever had before.

By the time I got to the big hill I was really huffing and puffing. My heart was racing. And with the wind blowing in my face, I was gulping air. By then I was way ahead of Jimmy and Sheila. *Who cares about the two of them anyway? Who cares that all of a sudden her stupid face doesn't make him feel sick!*

I struggled to make it to the top of the hill without slowing down. I was breathing as hard as I could when something flew into my mouth! I coughed. I gagged. I swallowed. *I think it was a fly! I think I swallowed a fly!* I gagged again and braked so fast I flew off my bike. Lucky for me I was wearing a helmet and landed in the soft dirt on the side of the road.

In a couple of minutes Jimmy and Sheila pulled up next to me and jumped off their bikes.

"What happened?" Jimmy asked.

"I swallowed something! I think it was . . . a fly."

"A fly?" he said.

"I was going really fast . . . breathing hard . . . it flew right into my mouth."

"How do you know it was a fly?" Sheila asked.

"What else could it be?" I said.

"A bee . . . a moth . . . a small bird."

"It wasn't a small bird!" I told her. "And a bee would have stung me. I'm almost sure it was a fly!"

"Eeeuuuw . . . that's so gross!" Sheila said.

I starting coughing and gagging again.

Jimmy whacked me on the back. "What should we do?" he asked Sheila.

"We'll take him to Bicycle Bob," Sheila said. "He'll know what to do."

"I think I'm going to puke," I said.

"No you're not!" Sheila said. "Just get back on your bike and keep your mouth shut!"

"Maybe he should keep it open," Jimmy said. "In case the fly wants to get out."

"It's too late for that," Sheila said.

"How do you know?" I asked.

"All right . . . fine," Sheila said. "Keep your mouth open if you want."

But I didn't want to. I was afraid if I did, something else would fly in.

The bike shop was just up the road. When we got there Sheila called, "Bob . . . we have an emergency!"

Bicycle Bob came out of his shop carrying a wrench. "Hey guys . . ." he said. "What's happening?"

"I was riding my bike really fast . . ." I told him. "I was breathing really hard . . ."

"A fly flew into his mouth," Sheila said.

"And he swallowed it," Jimmy added.

"Hey . . ." Bicycle Bob said, shaking my hand. "Welcome to the club!"

"The club?" I said.

"Yeah . . . the I.S.A.F. Club."

"The I.S.A.F. Club?" I repeated.

"The *I Swallowed a Fly Club*," Bicycle Bob said. "I'm a member myself."

"You swallowed a fly?" I said.

"I'm approaching the half-dozen mark," he said. "It's hard to pedal fast and keep your mouth shut at the same time."

"Does he need X rays?" Jimmy asked.

"Nah!" Bicycle Bob said. "He needs ice cream."

"Ice cream?" I said.

"Yeah . . . go next door to Ickle's and get yourself a vanilla cone."

"Why vanilla?" Sheila asked.

"It's the best cure for swallowing live insects," Bicycle Bob said. "Unless you don't like vanilla . . . in which case . . ."

"Vanilla's fine," I said.

"Good. You need money?"

"No. I've got enough."

"Then you're all set," he said. "Give me your name and address so I can notify you about our meetings."

"What meetings?"

"The I.S.A.F. Club meetings."

"Oh, right . . ." I wrote out my name and address for him.

Then the three of us went next door to Ickle's. I was glad Libby doesn't work mornings. She was the last person I wanted to see now. Tony Ickle, the owner's son, waited on us. I ordered a vanilla cone. Jimmy ordered a chocolate cone with sprinkles and Sheila ordered a strawberry.

"You're Libby's sister, aren't you?" Tony said to Sheila.

"Yes."

"Great girl, Libby . . ." he said.

You can't mean Libby Tubman, I thought. *You must mean some other Libby. Nobody in his right mind would call Libby Tubman great!*

"What a hunk!" Sheila said as we left the store with our cones. "No wonder Libby loves to go to work."

We sat in the little park next to Ickle's and ate

our ice cream. It felt weird to be eating ice cream at ten o'clock in the morning.

When we were done, Jimmy wiped his hands on his jeans and said, "Okay . . . I'm ready for the library."

We walked our bikes up the street but when we got to the library I said, "I'll wait out here."

"Don't you want to see Izzy?" Sheila asked. "Don't you want to tell her you swallowed a fly?"

"Somebody has to watch the bikes," I said.

"Nobody's going to steal our bikes," Sheila said. "This isn't New York City."

"Plenty of bikes get stolen here," I said. "Just read the local paper."

"Peter's such a worrier!" Sheila told Jimmy.

"I don't worry! I think ahead."

"Too bad you didn't think ahead before you swallowed that fly," Sheila said.

The two of them went inside. *They're probably going to tell Isobel about the fly!* I thought. *She'll probably come out to see if I'm okay. She'll remind me about that baseball book I put on hold. And if she looks at me the way she did the other day I'll get dizzy again. Then Jimmy and Sheila will know the truth . . .*

They weren't gone for long. "Izzy's not there," Jimmy said, disappointed. "She only works afternoons."

"Too bad!" I said.

"What's so great about swallowing a fly?" Fudge said that night. We were having an outdoor barbecue to celebrate the first warm night of our vacation. "One time I swallowed a turtle."

"We know," I told him.

"And I had to go to the hospital!"

"We know," I told him.

"Everybody was worried," he said. "And sad, too."

"Nobody was sad but me," I said. "Because it was *my* turtle!"

"I remember that turtle," Jimmy said. "You won him at my birthday party."

"Pul-eeese!" Sheila said. "Could we talk about something else? I'm trying to enjoy my supper."

Fudge laughed. "That's how Turtle got his name . . . right, Pete?"

"Yeah," I said. "I named my dog after my first pet to remind me of what you did to him!"

Fudge danced around, holding up a french fry as if it were my turtle. "Oh turtles are so tasty," he sang, "boiled, baked or raw . . ."

"Cut that out!" I yelled.

"You can't make me!" He laughed, daring me to try.

"Oh yes I can!" I reached out, grabbed him, then poured my whole cup of juice over his head.

He looked surprised. "Pete . . ." he cried, as the juice dripped down into his face. "How could you do that to me?"

"It was easier than I thought," I said.

Baby Feet

Mr. Fargo set up an outdoor studio in the side yard. He spread his canvas on the grass, like a rug. On Saturday morning, I saw him climb a ladder with a bucket of blue paint. When he got to the top he tossed it at his canvas.

So when Sheila screamed, "Mrs. Hatcher . . . come quick . . . Fudge is all blue!" I figured he'd gotten into Mr. Fargo's paint.

Grandma and Mom came running from one direction. Me and Jimmy from another. Fudge was sprawled out on the ground near his garden. His face was streaked with blue, his shirt was stained blue, his hands were blue, he had blue in his hair. Even his tongue, which hung halfway out of his mouth, was blue. "Mr. Fargo's going to go nuts!" I told Mom. "None of us are supposed to get anywhere near his art supplies."

"I don't think it's paint," Mom said, spying an empty fruit basket on the ground. She picked it up and waved it at Fudge. "Did you eat up all the blueberries?"

Fudge moaned.

"You ate our blueberries!" I said. "Jimmy and I were on our knees more than two hours picking them. And Grandma was going to bake us a pie!"

"I didn't eat them all," Fudge said, in a very small voice. "Turtle ate some."

"You fed Turtle blueberries?" I asked.

"He liked them."

"Turtle's a dog!" I said. At the sound of his name, Turtle appeared from behind the bushes. He plopped down next to me. "Let me see your tongue," I said, opening his mouth. *Blue! His tongue and teeth were all blue.*

Fudge clutched his stomach and moaned again.

"Boy, are you going to be sick!" Jimmy told him.

"I already am," Fudge cried. "My tummy hurts so bad!"

"I'm not surprised," Mom said.

"I know exactly what he needs," Grandma said, heading for the house. She came back with that peppermint medicine we get every time we have an upset stomach. "Down the hatch!" she sang, feeding him one teaspoonful.

"How about some for Turtle?" I asked.

"Why not?" Grandma said. "What's good for the goose is good for the gander." I held Turtle's mouth open and Grandma poured in a spoonful.

"Blue gas," Jimmy whispered. "He's going to make blue, steamy, gurgling gas."

"I don't want blue gas!" Fudge cried.

"What are you talking about?" Mom said. "There's no such thing as blue gas."

"There is if you eat enough blueberries," I told her.

"Really, Peter . . ." Mom said. "Let's not make this any worse than it already is."

Dad missed the blueberry adventure. He'd gone to the town dock right after breakfast to see about renting a sailboat. By the time he got back Mom had carried Fudge to the porch, where he lay on the old wicker couch. Everyone gathered around the blueberry boy. Everyone had a suggestion for him.

"Lie on your tummy, Fudge," Mrs. Tubman said. "That's what I do when mine hurts."

"A hot-water bottle," Mr. Tubman said. "That'll fix it."

"Make beautiful pictures in your mind," Buzzy Senior suggested.

"Just throw it all up!" Mr. Fargo said.

Sheila was about to say *Eeeuuuw . . . disgusting*, when Dad ran up the porch steps. "I've rented a nice little nineteen-footer!" he announced. You could tell he was really excited. "We can take a picnic lunch." He stopped when he saw Fudge. "What's wrong with Fudgie?" he asked Mom. "Why is he all blue?"

"It's a long story," Mom said. "I'll tell you about it later."

Dad paused for a minute and shook his head. Then he said, "Well . . . I've got the boat from noon to four and I can take up to six passengers. I know Peter wants to come . . . how about the rest of you?"

"I've never been sailing," Jimmy said.

"No problem," Sheila told him. "I'm an expert. I'll explain everything to you."

Somebody should tell the Guinness Book of World Records *about her*, I thought. *Since she's the world's leading expert on everything.*

"Count me in," Grandma said.

"Count me out," Buzzy Senior said.

"Buzzy . . ." Grandma said. "You don't like sailing?"

"About as much as a fish likes being out of water."

Mr. Fargo said, "Thanks, but no thanks."

Mrs. Tubman said she really wasn't into water sports, but she'd go if Mr. Tubman would. Mr. Tubman said he had no sailing experience but he'd always wanted to give it a try.

"What about Fudge?" Sheila asked Mom.

"Fudge isn't going anywhere!" Mom said.

"Except to the bathroom," Jimmy whispered to me. And we both cracked up.

All seven of us piled into the back of Mr. Fargo's truck. "Have a good sail!" he called when he dropped us off with our gear.

The boat Dad rented was tied to the dock. It looked kind of small, especially next to the really big boats that were moored in the harbor. As soon as we were on board Dad handed out life jackets. There was one for each of us and Dad's rule was we had to wear it the whole time.

Then he started to explain the *man-overboard* rule.

"Excuse me, Mr. Hatcher . . ." Sheila said, "but couldn't we call it the *person*-overboard rule? I mean, *man* overboard sounds so sexist."

"Okay," Dad said. "The *person*-overboard rule."

He appointed Mrs. Tubman and me official

spotters. If anyone fell into the water our job was to point. No matter how the boat turned, no matter how it rocked, the spotter had to keep pointing so the person overboard didn't get lost.

"Maybe I should just wait here," Jimmy said.

"Nah . . . once we get going you're going to like it," I told him.

"I don't know," Jimmy said. "I'm not the world's greatest swimmer."

"Nobody's going swimming," I said. "This water's so cold you'd have hypothermia in a couple of minutes."

"Hypo-who?" Jimmy said.

"Hypothermia," I said. "That's when your body temperature falls really low. Most people who die when they fall in the water die from that, not from drowning." I think Jimmy would have jumped back onto the dock if we hadn't sailed away right then.

"Oooh . . . my hat," Mrs. Tubman cried, as we got going. "The wind took my hat." We watched as it slowly drifted down into the water.

"Sorry, Jean," Dad said. "You should have pinned it to your hair."

"I didn't know," Mrs. Tubman said.

"Now you do," Dad told her.

"I really liked that hat," Mrs. Tubman mumbled. I don't think Dad heard her. He was at the tiller, which is the stick that steers the boat.

Soon we were moving along really fast, for a sailboat. I liked the *whoosh whoosh* sound as the boat cut through the water. Dad relaxed a little. So did the rest of us. We held our faces up to catch a few rays.

"Don't forget to use plenty of suntan lotion," Grandma said.

Sheila slathered it all over herself. By the time she was done she smelled like a coconut factory.

"I never burn," Jimmy told Grandma.

"Me neither," I said.

"Aren't you lucky!" Grandma said.

We sailed along that way for an hour before Dad called, "Anybody ready for lunch?"

"Yes!" we all answered at once.

We dropped the anchor near a small island. I handed out our lunch bags. Jimmy had brought his favorite—sardines and onions on rye. The rest of us had cold chicken, left over from last night's dinner.

"Am I hungry!" Jimmy said, gobbling up one sardine-and-onion sandwich and starting on the next.

"Me too!" Sheila said. "I've never been so hungry in my entire life."

"It's the salt air," Grandma said. "It does wonders for your appetite."

The three of us polished off a bag of chips, a

box of cookies and all the juice. Then we hit the fruit.

"Don't stuff yourselves," Grandma told us. "It's better to eat lightly when you're sailing."

"But we're anchored now," Jimmy said, helping himself to a second peach.

Grandma raised her eyebrows.

After lunch we relaxed for a while. Dad took a snooze. Grandma and Mrs. Tubman had a heavy discussion about the problems of the city. Mr. Tubman read a mystery. And the three of us played Hearts with the deck of cards Sheila had brought in her pack. "I'm always prepared," she told us.

After a couple of hands she said, "Speaking of prepared . . . is there a bathroom on this boat?"

"Look around," I told her. "Do you see a bathroom?" Since we were in an open boat it didn't take much to figure out the answer to that question.

"Well, what's a person supposed to do?" she asked.

"A person is supposed to go before."

"I did."

"Then a person is supposed to wait until we're back."

She checked her watch. "That's almost two more hours."

"If it's an emergency Dad has a bucket," I told her.

"A bucket?" Sheila said. "That's . . ."

"*Disgusting!*" Jimmy and I sang at the same time.

"Just when I think it's possible that the two of you are human beings, you prove that I'm wrong!"

Sheila's outburst woke Dad. He checked his watch. "We better get started. We'll be heading into the wind on the way back so it's going to take longer."

Once we were under way it felt a lot colder than before. We pulled on sweatshirts. Sheila shivered and moved closer to me. I moved away from her and closer to Jimmy. It got more and more windy as the sky filled with big gray clouds. The boat tipped and water splashed over the rail, spraying us.

That's when Jimmy grabbed my arm and said, "I feel funny."

"Dad," I called. "Jimmy feels funny."

"Keep your eye on the horizon," Dad told him.

"What horizon?" Jimmy asked. His eyes were rolling around in their sockets and he was turning green.

Grandma said, "Breathe through your nose,

Jimmy. Inhale, exhale . . . inhale, exhale . . ."

There were waves now, with white caps. The boat tipped *way* over and Sheila screamed, "Do something . . . before we all drown!"

"It's all right," Grandma said. "This is a keel boat. It can't go over."

It can't go over, I told myself. *It can't go over.*

Jimmy was trying to breathe through his nose, like Grandma said. I think he was more scared than sick.

"A puff is coming, Warren!" Grandma called.

"A puff of what?" Sheila cried, grabbing me.

"A puff of wind," Grandma said. "Look at the water . . . you see how it's rippling in front of us?" Then she shouted to Dad, "Warren . . . head up in the puff!"

All of a sudden the boat, which was already tipped halfway over, tipped so far the sails touched the water.

The Tubmans screamed and clung to each other. Sheila dug her fingernails into my hand. Jimmy groaned and hung on to me. He breathed his sardines and onions right into my face.

"Let Muriel take the tiller!" Mrs. Tubman yelled.

"You want Muriel to be captain?" Dad said. "Fine!"

"Really Warren . . ." Grandma said. "You're

overreacting!" But she switched places with him and took the tiller, shouting out orders. "Ease the sheets, Warren . . . we're going to sail off the wind . . . it may take a while longer but we'll all be more comfortable."

The boat straightened up and sailed more smoothly. Jimmy released his grip on me. So did Sheila. Her nails left marks on my hand. The Tubmans breathed more easily. And Dad sulked.

Grandma sailed the boat in like a pro. She explained everything as she did it, to make us feel more secure. "Now . . . as we pull up, Warren will jump onto the dock," she said. "And while he ties us up I'll drop the sail." She looked over at Dad. "Wait for me to give you the signal, Warren . . ."

But Dad didn't wait. He jumped too soon . . . and landed in the water!

"Person overboard!" Sheila shouted.

Mrs. Tubman and I remembered our responsibilities. We pointed at Dad. We pointed as some guy from the dock reached into the water and pulled him out. We pointed as someone else wrapped him in a blanket. We pointed until Dad looked at us and called, "Okay . . . th-th-that's enough! You c-c-can stop pointing now." He was shivering so hard his teeth clicked.

Mr. Fargo picked us up in his truck. As soon as we pulled into our driveway Sheila jumped out and ran for the house. "I have to go *soooo* bad!"

"Did you all have a nice sail?" Mom asked the rest of us. Then she noticed Dad. "Warren . . . how come you went swimming in your clothes?"

Dad didn't answer. "I'll be in the t-t-tub," he managed to say, heading for the house.

Mom looked at Grandma. "What happened?" she asked.

"Oh, the usual," Grandma said. "But all's well that ends well."

Fudge jumped off the porch steps. "All's well that ends well!" he sang.

"I see he's recovered," I said to Mom.

"More or less."

Then Tootsie toddled over and held her arms out to me. "Up, Pee . . . up."

I picked her up. She was barefooted and the bottoms of her feet were covered with blue. "Did you get more blueberries?" I asked Mom.

"No . . . why?"

"Look at Tootsie's feet."

"Oh oh," Mom said.

We ran to the side yard, where Mr. Fargo had left his work. Mom sucked in her breath when she saw the path of little footprints across his painting.

"What are we going to do?" I asked.

"What *can* we do?" Mom said.

Mr. Fargo and Jimmy came around the house then. Jimmy was telling him about his sailing adventure. "I was never scared," he said. "I knew it was a keel boat . . . I knew it couldn't go over." He stopped when he saw us and gave me a weak smile. "Peter wasn't scared either," he added.

But Mr. Fargo wasn't listening anymore. He'd seen the footprints across his painting. His face turned purple. I held Tootsie tight and waited for the explosion.

"Frank . . ." Mom began but Mr. Fargo held up his hand to stop her from speaking. He got down on all fours and crawled around his canvas. He stood up and walked away from it. Then he came closer. Then he walked away. Then he came closer again. He squinted. He scratched his beard.

We held our breaths.

Finally he muttered, "Baby feet."

I looked at Jimmy. He shrugged, as if to say *Don't ask me.*

"Baby feet," Mr. Fargo said again, coming toward me. I backed away. He wasn't getting his hands on my little sister.

"Itsy-bitsy baby feet," Mr. Fargo cooed. "Itsy-bitsy teensy-weensy baby feet." He tickled the bottoms of Tootsie's feet. She squealed.

Then he laughed. Mr. Fargo actually laughed! "How'd you like to be my partner, Tootsie Pie?" She held her arms out to him. He swung her up in the air. "I think we've got something here," he told her. "I think those little baby feet of yours are going to be a big hit!"

None of us knew what he was talking about but we were all relieved.

That night after supper, Jimmy and I used up a whole jar of Noxzema. We had sunburned faces, necks and ears. Our ears hurt more than anything. "Why didn't you use suntan lotion?" Mom asked.

"I never burn," Jimmy said.

"Famous last words," Grandma said.

Then Dad, who'd had supper in his room, came down in his robe. He clinked a spoon against a glass and said, "I'd like your attention for a minute."

Everyone looked at him.

"I behaved very badly this afternoon," he said. "And I want to apologize to everyone on the boat . . . but especially to Muriel . . . who saved the day."

"Apology accepted," Grandma said.

I was proud of Dad for admitting that he'd acted like a sore loser. So when he looked over at me I gave him the high sign and he smiled.

Then Mr. Fargo clinked a spoon against his glass. He stood up and said, "I want to thank Tootsie for walking across my canvas and giving me the idea for a series of paintings called *Baby Feet.*"

"Here, here . . ." Buzzy Senior said, raising his coffee cup. "Let's have a toast to *Baby Feet* and to Muriel, who always saves the day!" He gave Grandma a big kiss.

Grandma blushed. "Buzzy . . ." she said. "Not in front of the children."

Somehow I don't think Grandma was talking about us when she said *children*. I think she meant Mom and Dad and Mr. and Mrs. Tubman. Because they were the only ones who looked surprised by that kiss.

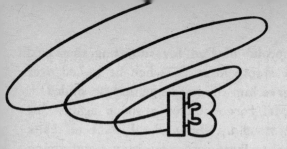

Captain Fudge

"Look at my *mitt-sy*," Fudge said early Sunday morning. The two of us were on the porch, waiting for Grandma to call us in to breakfast. She was making pancakes as a special treat.

"Doesn't it look good?" He handed his baseball glove to me. "Feel how soft it is."

"What'd you do?" I asked. There were dark splotches all over it.

"Oiled it, like the man in the store said."

"What'd you use?"

"Guess."

I sniffed his glove. There was a familiar smell to it.

"I'll give you a hint," he sang. "It's pink."

"Pink oil?"

"Yes!" he said. "You give up?"

"Yeah . . . I definitely give up."

"Oil of Olay." He gave me one of his satisfied smiles.

"You used Oil of Olay on your mitt?"

He nodded proudly.

"Oil of Olay is for skin, Turkey Brain! Mom uses it on her face."

"I'm not a turkey brain! You're the turkey brain and you're just jealous because your mitt's not as soft as mine."

"Yeah . . . right . . . and I'm jealous that my mitt doesn't smell like that pink stuff, too!"

"I *like* that smell."

"I'm glad . . . because you're going to be smelling it for a long time. What'd you do . . . use up the whole bottle?"

"The man in the store said to oil it every night . . . remember?"

"He said a few drops . . . and he was talking about neat's-foot oil."

"What's neat's-foot oil?"

"It's what you're supposed to use on a baseball glove."

I watched the expression on his face change as he got the message. "Never Oil of Olay?" he asked, in a small voice.

I shook my head.

Now he was about two seconds away from tears. *Why didn't I just tell him his glove looks great? Why'd I have to make such a big thing out of it?* So I said, "Look . . . it's not like you did anything wrong. You were just being . . . uh . . ." I paused, trying to find the right word.

"Creative?" he asked.

"Yeah . . . creative." I handed him his glove and went to see what Jimmy was doing.

He was still in bed, sound asleep. "Hey, Jimmy . . . wake up . . ."

He rolled over and buried his head under the pillow. "I'm not getting up today," he mumbled, curling himself into a ball.

I pulled the covers off him. "The ball game starts at 10 A.M."

"What ball game?"

"You *know* what ball game."

"Oh, that ball game. I'll probably strike out every time I'm up."

"So what?" I said. "It's not every day you get to play with Big Apfel."

"I never even heard of this guy until you started in on him."

"Too bad," I said, "because he's headed for the Hall of Fame."

"Says who?" Jimmy asked.

"Says me!"

There were more people at the high school field than I had ever seen in Southwest Harbor. And more dogs than I had ever seen anywhere, except in Central Park on a sunny day. Enough dogs for a team of their own.

When Sheila saw all those dogs, she screamed and ran back to her father's car. "I'll wait here!" she said, slamming the door.

"It's going to be a long wait," Mr. Tubman told her.

"I don't mind," Sheila said. "I brought a book, just in case."

"I thought you're not afraid of dogs anymore," I said.

"I'm not . . . once I know them. But strange dogs can give you diseases."

"Not if you don't kiss them," I said.

"Ha ha!"

"If you change your mind . . ." Mr. Tubman began.

"I'll never change my mind!" Sheila told him.

Mr. Tubman shook his head but he didn't force Sheila out of the car.

Jimmy and I headed for the field. I stopped in my tracks when I saw this great-looking girl in a red-striped T-shirt, stretching out near third base. *It was Isobel!* "That's her," I told Jimmy.

He gave me a blank look.

"Isobel . . . from the library," I said.

"Really?" Jimmy said. "That's Izzy?"

"Yeah!"

"She's incredibly ugly!"

"What are you, crazy?" I said. "She's beautiful!"

Jimmy slapped his thigh and laughed. "I got you that time," he said.

"Very funny," I told him.

There were other familiar faces, too. The woman who owns Oz Books was there. I call her Dorothy of Oz, even though that's not her real name. And the butcher, from Sawyer's Market. Bicycle Bob was there, too. He said, "So . . . how's the newest member of the I.S.A.F. Club?"

"Great," I told him.

"Keeping your mouth shut?" he asked.

"I'm trying."

"That's the way!" He cuffed me on the shoulder.

Suddenly a low murmur ran through the crowd. Everyone looked toward home plate. And there he was! Dressed in full Red Sox uniform. *Big Apfel . . . in the flesh!*

I recognized him right away. First, by his

height—six feet six inches without spikes—and second, because he still looks a lot like the picture on his baseball card. Except he's gained a few pounds and now his hair is gray.

Everyone gathered around him. You could feel the excitement. Mitzi and Fudge were right in the middle of it, each with an arm around one of Big's legs. I tried to work my way closer but I got shoved aside by the guy from the hardware store.

My heart was pounding. *Please let me be on his team,* I prayed. *I'll never ask for another thing if I can just play on his team.*

Then Big spoke and his voice boomed. "As most of you already know, these old knees aren't what they used to be. I can't take the field or run the bases anymore." He looked right at me and nodded, as if he knew me. "But I can still knock one out of here every now and then!"

I cheered with the crowd.

"So to be fair," Big continued, "I bat for both sides!"

Everybody cheered again. Everybody except me. "What?" I said. "How can he bat for both sides? That's impossible. That's against the official rules."

"*When in Rome . . .*" some woman, who was standing next to me, said.

I glared at her.

She glared back and repeated the whole phrase, as if I hadn't gotten it the first time. *"When in Rome, do as the Romans do."*

"I've got news for you," I told her, feeling my face turn hot. "We're not in Rome."

"And I've got news for you, *junior*," she said. "Rudeness will not be tolerated in this game!"

"Who's being rude?" I asked.

"Cut it out, Peter," Jimmy whispered, grabbing my arm.

I shook him off.

"Calm down . . . will you?" he said. "It's just a game."

"I suppose you think it's fair for him to bat for both sides."

"Yeah . . . I do."

I looked away. My throat felt tight.

Big grabbed a fistful of straws and everyone who wanted to be captain drew one, including Jimmy and me.

"Look . . ." Fudge said, holding up a short straw. "I'm captain!"

Isobel held up the other short straw. "I'm captain, too!"

"I can't believe this!" I said.

"Maybe she'll pick you for her team," Jimmy said.

"Yeah . . . sure." I wasn't about to admit I was hoping the same thing.

"Hey, Izzy . . ." Fudge called. "I'm writing that book. I'm already on Chapter Four."

"Fantastic!" Isobel called back.

"Let's go!" some guy with a serpent tattoo shouted. "Choose up sides! This is a ball game . . . not a social hour."

Captain Fudge, with his Oil of Olay mitt, got to choose first. So who did he pick? The biggest, strongest-looking player? No . . . that would have made too much sense. He chose Mitzi.

Then it was Isobel's turn. *If I were the Amazing Kreskin I'd be able to make her choose me.* I concentrated on my name, trying to get the message through to her. *Peter Warren Hatcher . . . Peter Warren Hatcher . . .* Isobel looked at me and smiled. *Yes!* I thought. *It's going to work.* I closed my eyes.

When I did, Isobel chose Tony Ickle.

Then Fudge picked me. *Good-bye, Isobel.* I tried to get him to choose Jimmy next, so at least I'd have a friend on my team. But did he listen? No! And Jimmy wound up on Isobel's team. Nothing was working out the way I'd planned. Absolutely nothing!

Our side took the field. *When in Rome* was on first base, I was on second, and Buzzy Senior was on third. Fudge and Mitzi stood right next to each other at shortstop. And Dad was on the mound.

Isobel's team lined up. Tony Ickle was their first batter. Dad threw a fastball but it was wild. He threw six more before he settled down. Lucky for us it's a no-walk game. Tony popped up the first one that crossed the plate. It came toward me.

I was ready for it but I took my eye off the ball—just for a second—just to make sure Big Apfel was watching. When I did, the ball dropped at my feet. I picked it up and panicked. My throw to first went over the head of *When in Rome.*

"Wake up, junior!" she yelled. "Where are your eyes . . . in the back of your head?"

I could feel everyone staring at me. I swallowed hard and blinked back tears. *If only I could do it over I know I'd make the catch.*

"It's all right, Peter . . ." Dad said. "We all make mistakes."

Sure, I thought. *But we don't all make* two *on the first play of the game.* My legs were shaking and I felt Grandma's pancakes bouncing around in my stomach.

Before the first half of the first inning was over Isobel's team had five runs and Big hadn't even come up. When he did, he slammed one out of sight and two more runs scored.

Finally it was our turn at bat. Bicycle Bob was

on the mound for Isobel's team and he put every pitch right down the middle. By the time I came up we had two on and two out.

Okay, I thought. *This is it. This is my big chance. I can make up for my errors now. All I have to do is concentrate . . .* I stood up to the plate. Bicycle Bob wasn't going to get anything by me. I could feel Big watching. I could feel him thinking, *This guy might have potential after all.*

Bicycle Bob wound up and threw the first pitch. I took a huge cut and missed, spinning all the way around.

"It's *Fudge-a-mania!*" Mitzi sang.

"No it's not," Fudge told her. "It's a strike!"

"Oh," Mitzi said, disappointed.

I took another swing and missed again.

"Keep your eye on the ball, Pete!" Fudge called. Just what I needed. My five-year-old brother giving me tips at the plate.

Bicycle Bob threw the next pitch. This time I was ready for it. I heard the *crack* of the bat as it connected with the ball. It was a good, strong shot. *But, wait! It was headed straight for Grandma, who was playing deep at third!*

"Run!!!" my team yelled.

I ran for first, trying to keep my eye on Grandma at the same time. I hoped the ball wouldn't knock her down.

But I worried for nothing, because Grandma

jumped with her glove held high. She made a fantastic catch. I was out. Isobel's team cheered.

Thanks a lot, Grandma!

Just when I thought things couldn't get any worse, they did. We were back in the field. Isobel came up to the plate. She's one of those players who wiggles the bat. Actually, she wiggles more than the bat but I tried not to notice.

She knocked a slow grounder right at Mitzi. But Mitzi knew what to do. She had her glove on the ground and her legs together so the ball couldn't get through. She stopped it. She picked it up. "Look!" she called, showing everyone. "I got the ball!"

"Throw!" we all yelled at her. She looked confused, then threw the ball to Fudge, who was standing right next to her.

By then Isobel was on her way to second.

"Here!" I yelled at Fudge.

But instead of throwing the ball he ran it over and personally handed it to me. By then Isobel was on her way to third.

"Throw, Peter!" Buzzy Senior yelled.

But I was scared I'd throw it away again. So I decided to fake a throw instead. And it worked! Isobel headed back to second. When she realized I still had the ball she turned and tried for third again. We had her trapped between the bases. There was only one sure way to get her out. So

I ran after her. It wasn't my fault she changed directions *again* and we collided, falling to the ground together.

"This isn't football!" she shouted. Then she stood up, brushed herself off and marched off the field.

"Yea, Izzy!" Fudge cheered.

"She's on the other team!" I told him. "You're supposed to cheer for me. I'm the one who tagged her out."

"Yea, Pete!" he and Mitzi cheered, jumping up and down. They were the only ones who did.

As if that weren't enough, in the final inning Jimmy hit a perfect double to left field. And Big shouted, "Way to go, son!" I thought Big wasn't supposed to root for either team. I thought he was supposed to stay neutral.

Finally, the game was over. Captain Fudge didn't mind that his team lost 26 to 8. Or that he struck out every time he came to bat. He and Jimmy yakked all the way home. They sang "Take Me Out to the Ball Game." They made plans for next Sunday's game.

"I thought you have to leave on Thursday," I said.

"Nah . . . my dad said as long as the weather's good we can stay a while longer."

"Great," I said, but I wasn't sure I meant it.

"Big says I have real potential," Jimmy told me. "He says I just have to build up my confidence. He says once I have confidence there won't be any stopping me. I might even be heading for the majors."

"Great," I said again. Now I knew how Dad felt yesterday, on the boat. Like a real loser.

"And it's all thanks to you, Peter!" Jimmy said, dropping his arm over my shoulder. "If you hadn't forced me out of bed this morning none of this would have happened. You're *really* my best friend!"

"And you're my *best* brother," Fudge said, planting a sticky kiss on my face.

Maybe I'm not such a loser, I thought. *Maybe today just wasn't my day. But next Sunday could be completely different. Next Sunday I might make a fantastic catch and hit a grand-slam home run! Anything's possible in baseball.*

This time, when Jimmy and Fudge started another round of "Take Me Out to the Ball Game," I sang with them.

Mom hit the shower as soon as we got home and when she came out, she called, "Fudgie . . . where's my Oil of Olay?"

"Mr. Zuman took it, Mom," Fudge said. Mr.

Zuman is the guy who picks up the trash twice a week.

"Why would Mr. Zuman have taken my Oil of Olay?"

"Because the bottle was empty." Fudge was tying a red bandana around Turtle's neck. All the dogs at the game wore bandanas.

"But it was a brand new bottle," Mom said.

"It was still empty, Mom."

"But you said you only needed a few drops . . . for Mitzi."

"Not Mitzi," Fudge said. "My *mitt-sy.*"

"Your what?" Mom asked.

"You know . . . my baseball glove."

"You used my Oil of Olay on your baseball glove?"

Fudge undid the bandana from Turtle's neck and tied it around his leg, instead. Turtle barked.

"You used *all* my Oil of Olay on your *mitt-sy?*" Mom asked.

"Right," Fudge said.

"I can't believe this!" Mom said to herself. "All my Oil of Olay."

"Olay . . ." Uncle Feather said, as Sheila came into the room. "Olay . . ."

"I didn't know your bird speaks Spanish!" Sheila said.

"He doesn't," I told her.

"But I just heard him say *olé.*" Sheila went over to Uncle Feather's cage and snapped her fingers. "Olé!" she sang.

"*Olay . . . olay . . .*" Uncle Feather sang back.

"You see?" Sheila said to me.

"It's not that kind of *olé,*" I said. "It's *o-l-a-y.*"

"How could you possibly know that?" Sheila asked.

"Believe me . . . I know!"

The Ring Bear

"Big news!" Mr. Fargo announced two days later. "My dealer in New York loves the idea of *Baby Feet*. I'm going to do a whole series of *Baby Feet* paintings. And when I'm done, there'll be a show at a gallery in SoHo. You'll all have to come." He picked up Tootsie and shook her. "We're going to be famous, Tootsie Pie!"

"How about rich, Dad?" Jimmy asked. "Could we get just a little bit rich while you're at it?"

"You never know," Mr. Fargo said. And for the second time that week, he laughed.

If Mr. Fargo gets rich on Tootsie's footprints, will Tootsie get something too? I wondered.

"That's wonderful news, Frank!" Mom said.

"Speaking of wonderful news . . ." Grandma said. She and Buzzy Senior stood with their arms around each other. "Buzzy and I . . ." Grandma looked at him and smiled.

"There's only one way to say it," Buzzy Senior said. Then he cleared his throat and began to sing: *"Who can explain it, who can tell you why?"*

Grandma joined him on the next line. *"Fools give you reasons, wise men never trrryyyy . . ."*

"Mother . . ." Mom said. "What are you trying to tell us?"

"Why Anne, dear . . ." Grandma said, "I thought it was obvious. Buzzy and I are in love. We're going to be married."

"Married?" Mom and Dad said.

"Married?" Mr. and Mrs. Tubman said.

"Yes . . ." Buzzy Senior said. "Married."

"Isn't this kind of sudden?" Mom asked.

"It may seem that way to you," Grandma said. "But at our age, sudden is okay. It's not as if we haven't met each other's families . . . is it?" She and Buzzy Senior laughed.

"When is this marriage going to take place?"
Mom asked.

"Oh . . . I don't know," Grandma said.
"Maybe tomorrow or the next day."

"Tomorrow?" Mr. Tubman said. "That soon?"

"Well, yes . . ." Grandma said. "While we're
all here together, in Maine."

"Couldn't you wait?" Mom asked.

"I suppose we could wait until next weekend,"
Grandma said.

Mom and Mr. Tubman looked like they were
in shock. I expected them to fall over any second.

"Grandpa . . ." Libby said, "what exactly does
this mean? Does this mean I'm going to be
related to the Hatchers?"

"Related?" I said. *"Related?"*

Sheila cried, "Grandpa . . . you can't do this
to me!"

And I cried, "Grandma . . . you can't do this
to *me!"*

Jimmy just stood there, laughing.

And Fudge looked confused. "So I don't have
to marry Sheila because we're getting related
anyway?"

"Right," Grandma said.

"I can't believe any of this!" Sheila wailed.

"Don't worry, honey," Fudge said. "I'll get
you some of Mitzi's monster spray."

"Well," Mr. Fargo said, "this calls for a toast! Didn't I see a bottle of champagne on ice?"

"Good thinking, Frank!" Buzzy Senior said.

So there's going to be a wedding in Maine after all. Except Sheila and Fudge aren't going to be the bride and groom. Grandma and Buzzy Senior are. I don't know how I feel about that. I mean, I like Buzzy Senior. And I'm glad Grandma's happy. But does this mean we'll have to spend every holiday with the Tubmans? Does it mean I'm stuck with Sheila as my *stepsomething* for the rest of my life?

That night everyone sat around making wedding plans. Even Mom and Mr. Tubman got involved. I guess it just took them more time than the rest of us to get used to the idea of his father marrying her mother.

"We want to keep it very simple," Grandma said. "Something informal . . . outside . . . under the trees . . ."

"Tees," Tootsie said.

"Yes, sweetie pie," Grandma said, "trees." She bounced Tootsie on her lap.

"Muriel . . ." Sheila said. "Can Libby and I be your bridesmaids?"

"I'd be honored," Grandma said.

"I've always wanted to be a bridesmaid!"

Sheila gushed. "But we need dresses . . . long, fluffy dresses . . . maybe pink or lavender."

"Oh, let's not bother with dresses," Grandma said.

"But all we have up here are jeans," Sheila said. "We can't be bridesmaids in jeans!"

"You can if you're creative," Grandma told her.

"What about me?" Fudge said. "I'm creative. Can I be a bridesmaid, too?"

"You can be the ring bearer," Grandma said.

"What's the ring bear?"

"It's like a bird breather," I told him.

"Really?" he asked.

"No," Mom said. "Peter's just being very silly."

"The ring bearer carries the rings," Grandma said. "On a pretty little pillow."

"What rings?" Fudge asked.

"The wedding rings, Turkey Brain. I thought you knew all about getting married."

"All I know is you get to sleep in the same bed."

"That's the best part," Buzzy Senior said.

Mom shook her head. "Really, Buzzy . . ."

Grandma and Buzzy Senior decided on a Saturday morning wedding so they wouldn't interfere with the Sunday ball game. Every time they went to town they invited someone else. Mom said they had to tell her how many people were coming, and soon. How else could she plan the wedding barbecue?

"Oh . . . just figure everyone is coming," Grandma said.

"Everyone?" Mom said. "What does that mean?"

It meant the guy from the hardware store, the butcher from Sawyer's Market, Dorothy of Oz, and the couple from the jewelry store, who sold them their wedding rings. It meant the Ickles from the ice cream parlor, Bicycle Bob, Isobel from the library and—Mitzi, Mrs. A and Big.

Mom worried about the weather but when we woke up on Saturday morning it was clear and warm. We all helped decorate the yard. We tied pink ribbons around the swing tree and set pots of pink flowers in Fudge's garden.

Sheila and Libby showed how creative they could be by sewing beads and ribbons all over their jeans and T-shirts. At the last minute Sheila decided we should dress up our animals, too. She tied a pink satin bow around Jake's neck. Then she asked me to tie one around Turtle's.

"You do it," I said. "I'm not that good with bows."

"I can't do it," Sheila said.

"Why not?"

"You know . . ."

"Because he's too smelly and disgusting for you to touch?"

"He's not that smelly anymore."

"Then why can't you do it?"

Sheila took a deep breath. "All right," she said. "I'll do it. But you have to hold him still."

I think Sheila's still scared of Turtle, but now that he and Jake are going to be stepdogs, she's making an effort to get along with him. Turtle wasn't crazy about having a pink satin bow tied around his neck. He tried to eat it.

Next, Sheila decorated Uncle Feather's cage. "Olé!" she said, snapping her fingers.

"Olay . . ." he answered.

The guests began to arrive at ten-thirty. Big wore his Red Sox uniform, but not his spikes. He gave Grandma and Buzzy Senior an autographed baseball for a wedding present. Mitzi brought them a bottle of monster spray, just in case. And she had one for Fudge, too. "Grandma just made it," she said, "so it's nice and fresh."

Actually, the bride and groom got a lot of interesting gifts. Matching bike helmets from Bicycle Bob. A book called *How to Survive Your First Year of Marriage* from Isobel. A set of hand-painted rocks from Sheila and Libby. A painting called *Baby Feet Go to a Wedding* from Mr. Fargo. The only copy in the entire world of *Tell Me a Fudge*, by Farley Drexel Hatcher. And a twenty-five-foot banner from Jimmy and me. We'd been working on it all week. It said:

WHO CAN EXPLAIN IT, WHO CAN TELL YOU WHY?
MURIEL AND BUZZY
AUGUST 28
SOUTHWEST HARBOR, MAINE

Grandma and Buzzy Senior liked it a lot, even though we forgot to include the year. Grandma said it was better that way.

Just before the ceremony Fudge asked Mitzi to help him be the Ring Bear. He showed her the lace pillow with the gold wedding bands resting on it. Then he whispered something in her ear and they giggled.

The judge was the last one to arrive. She pulled up in a shiny red pickup truck, wearing her judge's robe. She looked familiar. But I couldn't remember where I'd seen her until she said, "What are you doing here, junior?"

It was *When in Rome!*

"You're the judge?" I said.

"That's right, junior."

"My name is *Peter*," I told her. "Not *junior*. And my grandmother is the bride."

"Well, isn't that something!" she said. "I hope you behave yourself today."

"*When in Rome . . .*" I told her.

This time she laughed.

The ceremony began a few minutes after eleven. The bride wore a white jogging suit. She bought it at the sports store where Fudge got his *mitt-sy.* She had a pink flower tucked behind her ear. The groom wore a black jogging suit. He had a pink flower pinned to his sweatshirt. They kept smiling at each other.

When in Rome started off by reading some love poem. I almost laughed, because I had this picture in my mind of her playing first base in her judge's robe. Then she got down to the important stuff, like the *Do you take . . .* question. She asked Grandma first. "*Do you take this man to be your lawfully wedded husband?*"

Grandma said, "*I do.*"

After that Buzzy Senior was supposed to place the ring on her finger. But just as he was about to take it from the lace pillow, the Ring Bear and his helper sang, "Surprise!" And they started twirling, holding the pillow between them.

We were surprised all right. Because as they twirled, the rings flew off the pillow and landed somewhere in the grass. "Oh oh . . ." the Ring Bear said.

Everyone got down on their hands and knees to search.

"Suppose we can't find them?" Sheila asked. "Can Muriel and Grandpa still get married?"

"Don't worry," *When in Rome* said. "I'm here to marry them one way or another."

"Here's one!" Dorothy of Oz called, holding up a gold band.

It took a few more minutes before Bicycle Bob found the other.

"Okay," *When in Rome* said. "Let's give it another try. And this time, no surprises!" She looked at Mitzi and the Ring Bear.

"But surprises are fun!" Mitzi said.

"Next time you try that kind of surprise you're going to get a big surprise from me!" she told them.

They got the message.

On the second try everything worked. *When in Rome* pronounced Grandma and Buzzy Senior husband and wife. Then they kissed and everyone cheered. Well, almost everyone. A few people, like Mom, got teary-eyed.

The wedding barbecue was a huge success. Big helped Dad and Mr. Tubman tend the grills. Tony Ickle had brought gallons of ice cream. And Mrs. A had baked a blueberry wedding cake. So we all wound up with blue teeth. All except Fudge. He still won't go near a blueberry.

The party lasted for hours. Everyone was having too much fun to go home. Finally, the bride and groom fell asleep on lawn chairs. I knew how they felt because I was pooped out, too. Only the *Fudge-a-maniacs* were still going strong.

Sheila yawned and sat next to me on the porch steps. "Wasn't that the most beautiful wedding?" she asked.

"Yeah . . ." I said. "It was the best wedding I've ever seen." It was also the *only* wedding I've ever seen.

Sheila smiled at me. "I just want you to know, Peter . . ." she said, in her kissy-face voice, "that even if we are related, I'll always hate you."

"That's a relief," I said. "Because I'll always hate you, too."

"Promise?" she asked.

"Promise," I said.

"Let's shake on it."

I put out my hand.

She grabbed it.

Then we shook.